*Acclaim for*
Slaves of the Emp

"*Slaves of the Empire* is a dangerous, seductive nov.. ..... ... ... roads of erotic fantasy and political thriller. Travis arrays his characters—gladiators, slaves, Roman senators—in artful configurations, and then allows them to venture into charged sexual territory, taking the reader along for a journey that is sometimes unsettling, sometimes rapturous, and always gripping."

—Kilian Malloy,
*EDGEBoston*

"*Slaves of the Empire* is a hot, tense novel that pumps ancient Rome for all it's worth—rival gladiators and their magnificent spears, compliant eunuchs and their cleansing tongues, twin Germanic slave-princes and their sweet, abused nipples: depravity, depravity, depravity! With an artist's eye for detail and a historian's knack for accuracy, Aaron Travis had his way with me from the first sweaty page to the heart-stopping twist at the end. He's a real master in the best, most dominating sense of the word."

—Ed Sikov,
Author, *On Sunset Boulevard:
The Lives and Times of Billy Wilder*

"Since its original, serialized publication in *Drummer* magazine more than twenty years ago, Aaron Travis's *Slaves of the Empire* has gained near mythological status in gay male erotica. In a universe of sexy (and not so sexy) dross, Travis's work is pure gold. It is certainly sexy, and violent, but it is also smart, psychologically astute, and beautifully written. With the dangerous leanness of a James M. Cain noir crossed with the cathartic violence of a Japanese horror film, Aaron Travis taunts and goads us to places we long to go, but are afraid of imagining on our own.

*Slaves of the Empire* has all of the trappings of your typical sword and sandal porn fantasy, cruel senators, highly sexed gladiators, and nubile slave boys, but Travis brings this all to life with an energy, and an accumulation of salient psychic and emotional detail that stuns us. To call this, as some critics have, 'thinking man's porn' or even 'high-class erotica' is to miss the point. *Slaves of the Empire* is literature that is compelling, provoking, and sexually exciting. It is a high point of gay male writing in the second half of the twentieth century."

—Michael Bronski,
Author, *Pulp Friction: Uncovering
the Golden Age of Gay Male Pulps*

## NOTES FOR PROFESSIONAL LIBRARIANS AND LIBRARY USERS

This is an original book title published by The Haworth Positronic Press™, Harrington Park Press®, an imprint of The Haworth Press, Inc. Unless otherwise noted in specific chapters with attribution, materials in this book have not been previously published elsewhere in any format or language.

## CONSERVATION AND PRESERVATION NOTES

All books published by The Haworth Press, Inc., and its imprints are printed on certified pH neutral, acid-free book grade paper. This paper meets the minimum requirements of American National Standard for Information Sciences-Permanence of Paper for Printed Material, ANSI Z39.48-1984.

## DIGITAL OBJECT IDENTIFIER (DOI) LINKING

The Haworth Press is participating in reference linking for elements of our original books. (For more information on reference linking initiatives, please consult the CrossRef Web site at www.crossref.org.) When citing an element of this book such as a chapter, include the element's Digital Object Identifier (DOI) as the last item of the reference. A Digital Object Identifier is a persistent, authoritative, and unique identifier that a publisher assigns to each element of a book. Because of its persistence, DOIs will enable The Haworth Press and other publishers to link to the element referenced, and the link will not break over time. This will be a great resource in scholarly research.

# Slaves of the Empire

## THE HAWORTH POSITRONIC PRESS™
### Harrington Park Press®
### Greg Herren
### Editor in Chief

# Slaves of the Empire

Aaron Travis

The Haworth Positronic Press™
Harrington Park Press®
An imprint of The Haworth Press, Inc.
New York • London • Oxford

For more information on this book or to order, visit
http://www.haworthpress.com/store/product.asp?sku=5502

or call 1-800-HAWORTH (800-429-6784) in the United States and Canada
or (607) 722-5857 outside the United States and Canada

or contact orders@HaworthPress.com

Published by

The Haworth Positronic Press™, Harrington Park Press®, an imprint of The Haworth Press, Inc., 10 Alice Street, Binghamton, NY 13904-1580.

Previously published in 1985 by Alternate Publishing; in 1992 by Masquerade Books/Badboy Press.

PUBLISHER'S NOTES
The development, preparation, and publication of this work has been undertaken with great care. However, the Publisher, employees, editors, and agents of The Haworth Press are not responsible for any errors contained herein or for consequences that may ensue from use of materials or information contained in this work. The Haworth Press is committed to the dissemination of ideas and information according to the highest standards of intellectual freedom and the free exchange of ideas. Statements made and opinions expressed in this publication do not necessarily reflect the views of the Publisher, Directors, management, or staff of The Haworth Press, Inc., or an endorsement by them.

This is a work of fiction. Names, characters, places, and incidents either are the products of the author's imagination or are used fictitiously, and any resemblance to actual persons, living or dead, business establishments, events, or locales is entirely coincidental. This novel may contain scenes of graphic sex and/or violence. It is not the intention of The Haworth Press to condone any particular behavior depicted within this fictional work.

Cover design by Jennifer M. Gaska.

Library of Congress Cataloging-in-Publication Data
Travis, Aaron, 1956-
   Slaves of the empire / Aaron Travis.
      p. cm.
   ISBN-13: 978-1-56023-558-3 (pbk. : alk. paper)
   ISBN-10: 1-56023-558-6 (pbk. : alk. paper)
   1. Rome—Fiction. 2. Gladiators—Fiction. 3. Gay men—Fiction. I. Title.

PS3569.A96S59 2006
813'.6—dc22

                                                                    2005033931

# Preface

*Slaves of the Empire* was first published as a serial in *Drummer* magazine. This was in 1982, the rough-and-tumble heyday of gay publishing's erotic Golden Age, after the fall of censorship and before the advent of AIDS, when anything and everything seemed possible. I was twenty-six years old, and my muse dictated a steady stream of sexual fantasies that erupted in a plethora of short stories, novelettes, and one novel: *Slaves of the Empire*.

The novel was subsequently published as a trade paperback (illustrated by Cavelo), then as a mass-market paperback that went through multiple printings and appeared on *The Advocate*'s best-seller list (below Armistead Maupin's *Maybe the Moon* but above Madonna's *Sex*). The book was also translated into Japanese and German. This new edition marks the story's post-*Gladiator* reemergence in the twenty-first century.

*Slaves of the Empire* was obviously influenced by the sword-and-sandal movies of my boyhood. Growing up in a small town in Texas in the 1960s, I found escape at a drive-in theater that screened Hollywood epics like *Cleopatra, Ben-Hur,* and *Spartacus.* On Saturday afternoons, an independent Fort Worth TV station aired Sons of Hercules, a showcase of cheesy Italian movies about strongman heroes played by leading bodybuilders of the day, including Steve Reeves. There was always a lot of naked flesh, straining muscles, bondage, and sadomasochism in those movies, set against the exotic, pagan opulence of the ancient world. I loved them as a boy, and I still watch them occasionally.

Readers of a younger generation may have grown up without ever having seen one of those movies, and they may even have missed the reference in *Rocky Horror Picture Show* ("If you want something visual that's not too abysmal, we could take in an old Steve Reeves movie!"),

*Slaves of the Empire*
Published by The Haworth Press, Inc., 2006. All rights reserved.
doi:10.1300/5502_a

but they will almost certainly have seen *Gladiator,* a pastiche of previous sword-and-sandal epics which somehow won the Oscar. The cinematic allure of ancient Rome, particularly of the gladiator, lives on.

The erotic allure of the gladiator also lives on, as free as any Hollywood movie from the constraints of actual history. Although I have gone on to write serious historical fiction, *Slaves of the Empire* has no pretense of being historically accurate. When and where does the story take place? Nowhere, except in the imaginations of the author and his reader. The function of fantasy is to take us from one side of the looking glass to the other, and then (because it's only fantasy, after all) safely back again.

# PART ONE

# – One –

Magnus the gladiator ran the whetstone down the length of his long sword. Sparks flew from the glittering steel. Whetting blades was work for one of the attendants; but before a match, Magnus preferred to tend to this necessity himself.

He set the whetstone aside and pressed his thumb against the sword's edge. The blade could not be keener. Magnus sprang to his feet and swung the sword above his head, thrilled as a child at the sharp slicing wind of its passage through the air.

Magnus heard the distant roar of a thousand voices cheering. The sound erupted from the short hallway that led from the gladiators' quarters into the arena, signaling that the bout between Tardis and Urius had been decided. From the enthusiasm of the crowd's response, the victor had been the mob's favorite, the tall, fair-haired Urius.

Magnus frowned. He despised Urius. The young gladiator was hardly twenty, four years younger than Magnus, his smooth, sun-bronzed flesh as yet unscarred by the ravages of the arena. Urius was blond, with a shaggy straw-colored mane of hair cut in the Vandal style, square-jawed and clean-shaven with high cheekbones and heavy lips. He was handsome as Apollo, and a genius with the net and trident.

Urius was the new darling of the mob. The plebeians had begun to cheer for him almost as loudly as they cheered for Magnus—and to bet on him almost as heavily. The nobility had taken to inviting Urius to their private feasts; not long ago, only Magnus, of all the gladiators, had been accorded that privilege.

Though they often attended the same orgies, the two gladiators never spoke to each other, and never drank from the same passing wine cup. When they occupied the same room, they kept conspicuously apart, radiating opposing energies from their opposite corner:

*Slaves of the Empire*
Published by The Haworth Press, Inc., 2006. All rights reserved.
doi:10.1300/5502_01

Urius was light and Magnus darkness. They had both been favored by the gods; in a crowded room, the eyes of all others went back and forth between them. Urius was taller, but Magnus was more massive, his trunk and limbs as hard as hammered bronze. Urius's features were lean and classic; Magnus's face was broad with large, striking features, framed by the tangled curls of his hair and his beard. Where Urius was smooth as glass, jet-black hair washed over Magnus's broad chest and bristled across his massive forearms.

It was not the envy of a plain man for a handsome one that had made them enemies; it was their difference as men.

As Magnus had judged from the tumult of shouting, Urius had won his match. The young fighter came swaggering in from the arena and stood for a moment framed in the stone doorway of the gladiators' quarters, his trainer's arm reaching high to circle his broad shoulders. His arms and legs were covered with dust. A victory wreath was set about his sweaty brow, pressing the dark blond curls flat against his forehead. His bronze breastplate, molded to match the genuine contours of muscle and flesh, even to the details of nipples and a navel, was spattered with blood.

The other gladiators looked up from their chores and hailed him. Urius smiled wearily. He stood still and raised his arms as his trainer unlatched the straps of his breastplate. The heavy shield of bronze fell to the ground with a clatter, exposing his heaving chest. His broad, hairless pectorals and the deeply etched muscles of his belly were glossy with sweat; the golden flesh shone as smooth and hard as the sculptured plate of bronze that had protected him from Tardis's sword, and now lay in the dust covered with Tardis's blood.

His trainer withdrew. Some of the gladiators went back to their work, overseeing the slaves who were polishing their armor, or exercising on the dusty floor to loosen their muscles; but most, like Magnus, continued to watch Urius, knowing what would happen next.

Urius pulled his lips into a thin smile, showing a glint of straight white teeth. His eyes narrowed; his nostrils flared. A single bead of sweat clung to the tip of his broad nose.

He clutched the sheer, pleated skirt wrapped around his hips and tore it from his body. Beneath the skirt he wore only the leather cup that had protected his genitals during the fight. He unlatched the narrow straps of hide that circled his waist and threw the cup aside.

Urius then stood naked, except for the brown thongs wrapped around his forearms and hands, sandals on his feet, laced tightly to the knees, and the victory garland tangled in his long blond hair. His smoothly sculptured chest began to rise and fall, his eyes became glazed, as if he were in the heat of battle. His thick pale shaft, freed from the leather cup, at first hung heavy and bloated between his thighs, then began to jerk and stiffen until it stood upright, its blunt tip grazing the muscular depression above his navel.

"Zenobius!" he shouted.

Magnus ran his thumb down the blade of his sword and watched. One of the slaves who attended the common needs of the gladiators, a Syrian boy with black hair and olive skin, sprang up from polishing a shield and ran to the naked gladiator.

The slave Zenobius wore a very brief chiton, cut to reveal half his chest, and a chain around his neck. "Yes, lord," he said. His voice shook.

Urius narrowed his eyes and looked down at the boy. One corner of his mouth twisted into a smile. He took the base of his shaft between his forefinger and thumb and bent it down, pointing to a space on the floor before him.

"Kneel down, little pig."

Zenobius fell to his knees. He stared upward with wide eyes at the slick, rippling mass of Urius's torso, then dropped his gaze to Urius's shaft, now upright in the gladiator's fist. The long, pale sword of flesh was incredibly thick; Urius's hand could not encircle its girth. Zenobius stared at the shaft, and a shudder ran through him.

Magnus watched, as did all the gladiators, and clenched his teeth.

Urius tensed his body. A hundred muscles drew taut and quivered beneath the glaze of sweat. He ran his hands over his chest, coating them with sweat, and clutched his shaft with both fists. He closed his eyes, threw back his head and began to stroke himself.

The Syrian boy groveled at his feet, staring upward at the gladiator as if he beheld a god. He pursed his lips and pressed his thin brown hand between his legs, shaking with excitement. His eyelids flickered. His narrow chest began to rise and fall in time with the man who towered above him.

Urius roared like a wild beast. He pulled his hands away from his groin. He opened his eyes and looked down at his shaft. The massive pole of flesh shuddered. A jet of white cream bolted from the tip and landed with a liquid slap across the slaveboy's face, from his forehead to his chin, some of the liquid entering his open mouth. Zenobius writhed in the dust, eyes barely open, eyelashes clotted with white, as the gladiator's mallet danced in the air and painted his face with semen.

Urius smiled broadly and planted his fists on his hips. His chest heaved. His body glistened with a fresh sheen of sweat.

"Kiss it, pig."

Zenobius moaned. He leaned forward and touched his lips to the tip of Urius's rod.

"Little pig," Urius muttered. He slapped the boy's face. He drew back his hand, wet with semen, and slapped the boy again. Zenobius moaned and clutched the gladiator's thighs.

He leaned forward and kissed the tip of Urius's shaft.

Urius struck him again. The boy was knocked to the ground. He whimpered and crawled forward on his belly to kiss the gladiator's feet. Urius kicked him aside and strode toward the trough of water at the end of the long chamber. His shaft swung before him, slapping heavily against his thighs.

"Come, pig, I'm not done with you yet," he called, crooking his finger over his shoulder, not bothering to look back. "Come clean the sweat and dust from my body. Come and lick me, little pig!"

Zenobius rose shaking to his feet and followed in a daze.

Magnus clenched his teeth and curled his lip. Urius disgusted him. All the gladiators needed sexual release after a death match. Magnus knew the sensation well enough—the red haze of lust, the erection that would not subside, the overwhelming need to feel himself swallowed in flesh. After a kill, most of the gladiators had the modesty to retire to one of the private cubicles that lined the quarters, where they could be as demanding of the attendants as they wished without subjecting the boys to the added humiliation of being watched. Urius insisted on doing it in front of all the athletes, as if demonstrating that the power of his shaft were another part of the performance. He would probably do it in the arena, Magnus thought, spattering his semen on the corpse of his victim, if the gamemaster would allow it.

Urius was an exhibitionist, vulgar and conceited. He liked nothing better than for all the gladiators to see him, naked and smeared with blood, his muscles swollen from the exertion of the fight, with one of the boy attendants at his feet, groveling before his shaft.

Urius was large between the legs; larger than any of the other athletes, including Magnus. He was vain about his body—the sculptured mass of his arms and legs, the breadth of his shoulders and chest, the stonelike hardness of his belly—but even vainer about his shaft, aware of the edge it gave him over the other men. He displayed it proudly; he called attention to it constantly. He was often naked in the gladiators' quarters, usually more erect than flaccid, reaching down to stroke himself in the middle of an ordinary conversation, keeping his shaft big and swollen, observing with a smirk the intimidation he could achieve with a subtle reminder of the thing he carried between his thighs.

Once Magnus had asked him, in the first days of their acquaintance when he did not know Urius's nature and still thought they might become friends, why he preferred the trident over the sword. "My sword is between my legs," Urius replied, licking his lips, smirking lewdly as he gently raised his hips and touched himself. "It hasn't yet killed a man—but it has drawn blood, more times than I can count." His shaft was almost instantly erect.

That was the way Urius thought of his shaft, and the way he used it—as a weapon, to punish, to penetrate, to command. It was a potent weapon. There was no denying that. Even now, Magnus could hear the sounds of gagging from the far end of the room. He did not bother to turn and look. He knew what he would see: Urius, sitting on the edge of the trough with his massive thighs spread apart, holding the

Syrian's curly head in his hands and spearing the boy's throat with his newly hardened shaft.

Magnus heard the bark of the announcer's voice from the arena. He listened, glad of the distraction. Cleon and Philip, the two Greeks, were next. He watched them gather their weapons and head for the arena. Magnus liked them both. It was unfortunate that one would have to die today.

After that match, there would be a wild-beast spectacle; the gamemaster was ready to debut his latest acquisition, a rhinoceros from upper Egypt. There was a rumor, probably untrue, that a woman would be forced to copulate on its horn.

Then the sand would be swept clear for the chariot race; and after that, Magnus would be called for his match with the Nubian, the climactic fight of the day, the event that everyone had come to see. The Nubian was new to Rome, an import from Alexandria, where the crowds were said to adore him. Magnus had had only glimpses of the challenger; the Nubian was being kept apart, in his own quarters. All Magnus had been able to see was that the man seemed to have been hewn out of black marble, hard and smooth and shiny everywhere, even on his shaven head. The Nubian was tall, even taller than Urius. Magnus was confident, but apprehensive; they would both be using swords, and the Nubian had long arms.

The sound of rhythmic slapping, quick and sharp, drew Magnus back to the present; Urius was slapping Zenobius's face with his shaft and laughing. Magnus wished that he had been scheduled to fight Urius, instead of the Nubian. Then Urius would be dead today, an end put to his vile strutting and crass displays.

It would be at least two hours before he would be called to fight the Nubian. Magnus closed his eyes and clenched his fists, wishing the time would fly, wishing his own erection, cramped and bent inside his leather cup, would subside. His staff was always hard on the days he fought, from the moment he woke, even without the stimulus of watching Urius torment the Syrian slave. He knew, from long experience, that it would remain hard until the fight itself, when all his lust to pierce and penetrate would be drawn from his shaft into his sword.

A few times, he had given in to the need to relieve the tension between his legs before a match. Such indulgence was dangerous; it drained him of energy, and of the drive to stab and kill. On those days he had fought poorly, and once had come very close to being killed himself. It was better to wait, despite the burning need. Afterward, there would be relief, in the mouth or ass of one of the attendants.

Which of the slaveboys would he use today? Certainly not Zenobius, though he had used the boy before and been pleased. The Syrian would be half-dead by the time Urius finished with him. Magnus could hear the slaveboy now, groaning loudly. He turned, unable to stop himself from looking.

Zenobius was on his back in the dust, naked. His chiton had been ripped from his body and lay in tatters beside the trough. His lean brown legs were in the air. Urius was atop him, driving his shaft into the naked boy with long, vicious strokes, holding the boy's head up by the chain around his throat, slapping him and spitting in his face, laughing crudely. A small circle of gladiators stood and watched, groping themselves and exchanging lewd comments.

Magnus looked more closely. There was a strange, shifting expression on the slaveboy's face, vacillating from slap to slap between utter submission and intense shame. His face was like a clay mask, battered by Urius's hand. At one moment, the mask showed pain and humiliation—then Urius would strike it as he stabbed the boy with his shaft, and the mask was reshaped into an expression of craving and worship. Over and over Urius slapped the boy, until Zenobius's face began to twitch out of time with the blows, to draw tense and fall slack; his lips were broken, his cheeks were dark with bruises. The mask became unreadable, hardly human, almost frightening.

Urius suddenly pulled his shaft from the boy's ass and stood. His legs shook; his chest heaved. He looked down at the hard, glistening mass of his sex and smiled.

Zenobius remained for a moment on his back with his legs in the air, panting, staring hard at the gladiator's shaft. Then he lowered his legs and rolled forward onto his hands and knees. Urius retreated, taking small backward steps, flexing the muscles in his groin so that his shaft bobbed obscenely in the air. Zenobius crawled after him, his bruised mouth open wide, whimpering with lust, never taking his eyes from Urius's sex.

Urius stopped his retreat. Zenobius caught the waving shaft between his lips and drew it down his throat. Urius pursed his lips and hissed with pleasure.

Magnus looked away, disgusted. The boy was ruined for him. He could never use the Syrian again. Urius had polluted him. Magnus turned his back on them both, clutching the swollen mass inside his leather cup.

A crowd, larger than the group surrounding Urius, had gathered at the entrance of the gladiators' quarters. The rhinoceros had been led into the passageway. The beast was stamping its hobbled feet and snorting. A frantic Egyptian, evidently the animal's master, was shouting for the crowd to step back. The athletes, trainers, and attendants, overcome by curiosity, ignored his warnings.

Suddenly the rhinoceros thrashed its head, swinging its powerful horn within a hair's breadth of smashing the Egyptian's skull. The crowd gasped and scrambled back. Magnus laughed, glad again for anything to distract him from thoughts of sex.

Then a figure stepped through the crowd: a short, very muscular young slave with blond hair. The boy seemed oblivious to the commotion surrounding the rhinoceros; he appeared to be looking for someone in the gladiators' quarters.

Magnus recognized the young slave, and his thoughts were instantly wrenched back to the ache inside his leather pouch.

It was Eskrill—or Erskin, Magnus could not tell which—one of the twins owned by the senator Marcellus. It was said that the twins had been Germanic princes, warriors of the dense Northern forests, captured and enslaved by the general Silvius in his spring offensive. On his return to Rome, the general, knowing but not sharing Marcellus' sexual tastes, had given the boys to the senator as a gift in return for his political support of the war.

The two youths had excited great comment when Marcellus had presented them at a dinner party earlier in the season. Magnus had been a guest at the party. He remembered quite clearly the moment he had first seen the twins, kneeling at either end of the senator's divan, feeding their master grapes and quail's eggs with their fingers.

The brothers were identical, exactly matched in every feature. It was almost unthinkable that two faces could be so extraordinarily beautiful. There was innocence in their pale blue eyes and perfectly regular features, in the softness of their sunbrowned cheeks, and something about their mouths, wide with sensuous, deeply colored lips, could tempt a man to spoil that innocence. Their hair was blond, that pure yellow tint seen only among the Northern races, falling across their smooth foreheads in tight curls.

That night, at Marcellus's party, the boys had been virtually naked, decorated rather than dressed—chokers of gold around their necks, golden bracelets on their ankles and wrists, small pouches of blue silk tied about their genitals with gold wire. They were rather short, but dramatically proportioned, with broad, square shoulders, thickly muscled arms, flat bellies, and narrow hips. Their pectorals were naturally large and sharply defined, thick slabs of muscle with a sleek, hard cleft between.

Their calves and thighs were unusually developed, flowing upward into large muscular buttocks, smooth as white porcelain, full and round with a deep crevice between. Their posture, when they stood, invited every shade of lust: shoulders back, chests raised, legs apart— the high, hard shelf of their pectorals predominant in the front, the smooth, spherical thrust of their asses predominant behind.

Magnus had ached to touch them that night, to fill his hands with their firm breasts and cheeks, to taste their large brown nipples with his teeth and explore with his fingers the deep shadow between their buttocks. But the party had not offered the opportunity; Marcellus had kept the boys to himself. They had not been seen in public since that night, but Magnus had thought of them often.

Now one of the boys had entered the gladiators' quarters. He stood in that seductive posture, back arched, arms at his sides, scanning the chamber with his eyes. He wore a blue chiton, cinched at the waist by a thin leather cord, cut from a fabric so sheer that Magnus could probably have held the entire garment crumpled in one fist. The chiton left the right side of the slave's chest exposed, and was barely long enough to conceal his testicles and the bottom curve of his ass. The golden bracelets that marked him as Marcellus's slave were tight around his throat and wrists.

The boy's eyes fell on Magnus. He averted his gaze and approached the gladiator warily. Despite his reserve, it was the boy who spoke first.

"You are Magnus the gladiator, property of Harmon the merchant?" The boy's Northern accent was atrocious.

"Yes. And which one are you?"

The boy looked at him blankly, as if his Latin were not sufficient for him to have understood.

"What is your name, boy?" Magnus said sharply.

"My name is Eskrill. And you are the gladiator Magnus?"

"I am."

Magnus could not resist the urge to reach out and touch the boy's naked pectoral. He cupped the hard slab of muscle in his hand. The boy's flesh was smooth as silk. He lightly pressed his thumbnail against the boy's nipple.

Eskrill winced slightly, but did not draw away. Magnus was puzzled—and intrigued—by the display of sensitivity. He ran his fingertip around the aureole and discovered a ring of faint scabs, almost healed. Curious, Magnus pushed the strap of the chiton from the boy's shoulder.

The garment fell silently and the slave stood naked above the waist. The boy's nipples were out of symmetry. The one left bare by the chiton was marred but healed; the one that had been hidden was freshly molested, swollen and flushed, the skin mottled with patches of pink.

Magnus felt a surge of lust, an impulse to pull the cord from the young slave's waist and let the chiton fall, so that he could see him naked. But if he did that, he would be unable to resist proceeding further—his energy would be spent, the boy's owner would be furious. Magnus withdrew his hands. The boy began to pull the strap back into place across his shoulders, but Magnus gently deflected his arm; he wanted to look at the boy.

"My master would speak with you," Eskrill said.

"Now? What does Marcellus want with me?"

The boy looked at him warily, "My master sent me to fetch you," he said cautiously, as if he were afraid the words might give offense. Again, he attempted to cover himself; again, Magnus knocked his hand away.

"Where is he?" Magnus said.

The boy gestured with his chin: above, in the stands.

Magnus looked at the boy's swollen nipple. Some of the marks suggested the smooth curving bite of fingernails; others might have been the impressions left by a man's teeth. Where else had Marcellus left his marks on the boy? Eskrill's reserved manner was certainly not that of a young warrior from the barbarous North. A few weeks in Marcellus's thrall had rendered him submissive and subdued. There was no imagining the indignities the boy had been subjected to. Gladiators, Magnus knew, were known for the cruelty of their natures, the harshness of their sex; but there were those among the senators, each the petty tyrant of his villa outside the city, whose appetites were far more savage.

"Very well," Magnus said. "Lead me to him." He allowed the boy to pull the strap of the chiton over his shoulder.

The boy turned. Before he could take a step, Magnus took up his sword and gave the slaveboy a playful, impulsive slap across the cheeks. The boy jumped and looked over his shoulder with startled eyes. He reached behind and rubbed his hand over the place where the sword had stung him.

Magnus laughed, but the boy's expression stopped his laughter. There was a look of hurt in Eskrill's blue eyes, together with a passive acceptance that make Magnus' thoughts run wild. The boy's face reminded him of Zenobius's face when Urius had slapped him—not nearly so wild and uncontrolled, but the shame was there, and the craving as well, mixed together into an alloy that was both saddening and seductive, corrupt and irresistible.

"Go on!" Magnus barked. If he had to look at the boy's face for another instant, he would not be able to stop himself.

Eskrill led him through the crowd still gathered around the stamping rhinoceros, down one of the side corridors, and up a flight of steep, narrow steps that led upward into sunlight. Magnus watched the muscular workings of the boy's sturdy thighs and calves as he mounted the stairway. From his place behind and below, he could see beneath the hem of Eskrill's chiton.

Marcellus had beaten the boy, perhaps as recently as that morning. A thatch of welts ran across the lower portion of each pale cheek, the marks of a wooden cane or a thin strop of leather. Magnus's fingers flinched with the impulse to reach up and touch the marks, to trace the raised pattern they made across the firm, silky flesh. The welts looked fresh enough to still be warm.

They were alone on the stairway. It would be easy for him to push the boy to his knees on the steps, pull the chiton up over his ass and take him. He pictured the boy like that, crushed against the sharp stone, thighs spread apart, his face turned back in fear—teeth clenched, gasping as Magnus entered him. . . .

The fantasy clouded his mind—then they were clear of the steps, standing in sunlight and surrounded by the noise of the spectators. The boy turned and led him along the walkway that ran between the inner wall of the arena and the lowest tier of seats.

Magnus heard his name, spoken and shouted by the mob. Eskrill, too, was noticed—"and look, he's with one of Marcellus's new toys! The senator is a fool to trust Magnus with that one." There were whistles, laughter, shouts of "Hail, Magnus!" from the more serious spectators, and a drunken voice that yelled, "Fuck him, Magnus! Show us how you fuck the boy!" Magnus saw that Eskrill was blushing; his ears and the back of his neck turned deep red.

They walked a quarter of the way around the coliseum, past a file of soldiers and into the section reserved for the titled classes. The senator Marcellus sat alone in the third row, near the aisle, with an empty seat on either side.

Eskrill walked up the steps and past Marcellus, taking the seat at the senator's right. The short chiton pulled up as he sat, so that his welted buttocks pressed naked against the cushion.

Magnus waited in the aisle. "The slave says you wish to speak to me, Senator."

Marcellus did not look up, but indicated the cushion to his left. Magnus sat.

The senator took a sip of wine, looking shrewdly at Magnus above the rim of his goblet. Marcellus was a large man. The formless toga he wore did not conceal the immense breadth of his shoulders and chest. His body was still hard from his years as a general of the legions in Spain. His short black hair was touched with silver at the temples. His nose was large, but did not dominate his face. People remembered his eyes, gray and piercing, his large, square jaw, and his mouth, a straight grim line that seldom changed expression.

Marcellus lowered the goblet. "Would you like some wine, Magnus?" Even when asking a question, he sounded as if he was issuing an order; his cultured, brassy orator's voice had been hardened to steel by his years as a general.

"You're generous, Senator. But I must refuse. Not before the fight."

Marcellus nodded. "Of course." He looked away, into the arena, where the match between Cleon and Philip had been decided. A body was being carried out. Magnus could not tell which. The rhinoceros was being led in.

Marcellus looked again at Magnus, and seemed almost to smile. "I trust my slave had the good manners to introduce himself to you."

"Yes," Magnus said. Below, the Egyptian and several assistants were removing the hobbles from the rhinoceros's legs. "He seems to be quite well mannered, for a barbarian."

"Thank you. It was not easy training him, I assure you. He and his brother were very insolent when I received them from Silvius. They seemed to think they were still warriors—lazy, disobedient, much too proud. They tended to glower at me; it was not an expression suitable for their handsome faces, so I decided to change it to something . . . more pliable." He took a sip of wine.

"It tried my imagination, Magnus, thinking of ways to prove to them that they were no longer free men, no longer men at all, really, but slaves. *My* slaves. I don't think they knew what the word meant; perhaps their tribe does not practice slavery—that is sometimes the case among the lower races. I explained to them that I owned them,

just as I might own a horse—but that I would expect much more than
an occasional ride upon their backs."

Marcellus placed his hand upon the boy's thigh. Eskrill flinched
and remained tense. Marcellus's voice returned at a lower pitch.

"They have other strange habits in the North. They dress themselves in trousers and furs, the men as well as the women. For the cold,
of course; but it is insanity to cover legs like these, don't you think?
Polished metal and nude flesh are the only suitable clothing for a boy
such as this. They did not take to nudity. They found it unnatural and
embarrassing." Marcellus shook his head slightly and took a sip of
wine. "So selfish with their bodies—so many things they swore to me
they would never allow, so many acts they simply would not perform.
All that is changed now. I'm sure the details of their conversion would
only bore you."

Magnus glanced beyond the senator, at the boy, who sat stiffly,
staring down into the arena. The rhinoceros had begun stamping
about the field, smashing through barriers of wood as thick as a man's
chest.

"You speak of the slave as if he were not here."

"He understands very little of what we say. I'm afraid that he and
his brother, beautiful as they are, are not very bright. The Latin language is too complex, too sophisticated for them. But I have managed
to teach them to recognize certain words, to obey certain commands,
as one might teach a dog. Their speaking vocabulary is limited, but
interesting. They have learned how to beg. And they don't need Latin
to whimper."

The grim line of his mouth twisted at the corners. The senator was
smiling. "I was afraid the little mule would bring me the wrong gladiator. But I see that my instructions were specific enough. 'Fetch me
the tall, dark, handsome one,' I told him. 'The one with the thunder-
ous shoulders and soulful eyes.'"

Magnus shifted in his seat, frustrated by the senator's monologue,
by the nearness of the boy with Marcellus between. "Did you call me
here to pay me compliments, Senator?"

The thin smile faded, but Marcellus seemed more amused than before. "I called you here to discuss this slave, and his brother. I have a proposition to put to you."

"Yes?" Magnus's heart quickened in his chest. He glanced at Eskrill again and squeezed his leather cup without thinking.

The boy continued to stare into the arena. The agitation of his eyes belied the tranquility of his profile. He knew he was being observed and discussed; clearly, his grasp of Latin was greater than Marcellus acknowledged.

"The Northern stock, despite its backwardness, produces on occasion extraordinary specimens of masculine beauty," Marcellus said, "Eskrill is proof of that, don't you agree?"

"Yes," Magnus said. His mouth was dry. He thought of taking Marcellus up on his offer of wine, then decided against it.

"His nipples," Marcellus said, returning his gaze to the slaveboy. "Have you noticed how large they are, how they protrude, soft and swollen, from the hard slabs of muscle beneath? They are extremely sensitive, as sensitive as a girl's." He lowered his voice, almost to a whisper. "One night . . . one night I tied his arms behind his back, and Eskrill and I made love, the two of us, using only my hands and my teeth, and his nipples. He was unaccustomed to the pleasure. He spat at me. He twisted in his bonds and cursed me in his crude tongue. Slowly the curses turned to babble, then to whimpers, then to screams, and finally to weeping. He cried until his face and chest were wet with tears. Finally, he begged me to stop, but he was begging for the wrong thing. By morning I had only to breathe upon his nipples to make him weep. That was the night he learned to call me lord. The night he learned to beg for my shaft in his mouth."

Marcellus touched his fingernail to the tip of Eskrill's nipple. The boy stiffened, drew his eyebrows together and parted his lips.

"He has a large mouth, don't you think? But his throat is tight. His ass . . ." Marcellus did not finish the sentence, lost for a moment in thought. "They were both virgins when Silvius gave them to me. Neither had so much as taken a woman. Perhaps a goat." Marcellus laughed dryly. "They will never know a woman now, unless I decide to breed them. It might be pleasant, having their sons to amuse me when their own beauty grows dim.

"They had a curious revulsion for their own sex. They swore to me that no man's rod would ever pass their lips. They were astonished when I explained that it was not their pretty mouths which interested me most."

Marcellus put his middle finger into his goblet and pulled it out, red with wine. Eskrill stiffened. Marcellus slid his hand between the cushion and the boy's buttocks. Eskrill gasped softly as the finger entered him.

Marcellus turned to Magnus. "I had to break them. I had to strip them naked, chain them, put collars around their necks, beat them, starve them. They were very brave, my little princes. But in the end, it was their loyalty to each other that proved their undoing. I learned that neither could bear to see the other in pain. Their love for each other finally crushed their resistance. It was sad to break the spirit of a wild, beautiful boy, almost tragic; but a greater tragedy to let such perfection go to waste."

He turned back to Eskrill and spoke into the boy's ear in a low voice. "Tell me, slave, what do you think of this gladiator?"

Eskrill did not speak. He sighed as the finger churned inside him.

"Magnus is a great man," Marcellus whispered. "He is a slave, like yourself, but he is the idol of many a free citizen, envied even by nobles. A few years ago he was a mere galley slave on one of the trading vessels owned by the merchant Harmon. That explains the massive strength of his shoulders and arms. Then, so the story goes, Harmon caught a glimpse of the thing between Magnus's legs, and decided that Magnus was better suited for ploughing than for rowing. So the merchant took the galley slave into his home, and Magnus became the old man's stud. Are you listening to me, boy?

"Eventually Harmon turned Magnus out of his home—there was a scandal, I believe, something about a pregnant daughter—and put him to work as a gladiator. He has killed more than forty men in this arena and received hardly a scratch in return. He is young, though not quite so young as you; handsome, as handsome as you. Magnus is a slave, but he is also a man. The hair is thick on his chest. There is not a woman? in Rome who would refuse him in her bed, and many a man who would gladly kneel in worship before him. They say his shaft would not look out of place on a horse—very potent, very thick. Would you like to be used by this man?"

Eskrill bit his lip, then quickly released it, trying to hide his distress as another finger was pushed into his ass.

"Answer your master, slave." The words were cool but threatening, spoken through clenched teeth. "Or do I have to beat you for the second time today, here before all Rome?"

Eskrill sighed and closed his eyes. "Yes, lord, I would like to be used by this man."

"Would you like him to use your mouth? To choke you with his sex? Think of it. Think of its thickness in your throat."

"Yes."

"And your ass. Your beautiful ass that you force me to cover with welts because of your stubbornness. It would make you happy to take this gladiator's rod in your ass, to have him mount you and ride you like a squealing pig?"

"Yes."

Marcellus nodded gravely and smiled his grim smile. He pulled his fingers from Eskrill's ass and wiped them across the boy's lips. Eskrill wrinkled his nose and jerked his face away.

Marcellus's smile vanished. "You will be punished for that," he said flatly. He turned back to Magnus.

"That is my proposition to you. I have wagered a great deal on your victory in the match with the Nubian today. Because of that—and for certain other reasons—it is very important that you win the contest. Win it, Magnus, and I will give you a night with this slaveboy and his brother."

Magnus looked from Marcellus to the boy. "Both of them, together?"

"At my villa, tonight."

"Alone with them?"

"The three of you in a sealed room. You will own them for the night."

There was something suspicious about the senator's offer. Bribes were sometimes offered to a gladiator to lose a match, when the stake was not death; rewards were regularly given to encourage the athletes to continue fighting. But it made no sense to offer a bribe to win a death match. Magnus would be fighting for his life; there could be no greater inducement.

"You seem doubtful, Magnus. Perhaps you do not want the boys."

Marcellus lifted the skirt of Eskrill's chiton and folded it back, exposing the boy's genitals. Eskrill's hands flinched, but he did not move to cover himself.

Magnus stared. The slave had been shaved between his legs.

Marcellus ran his fingers lightly over the denuded flesh, smooth as glass, at the base of the boy's shaft. Eskrill began to grow erect. His eyes were tightly shut, his brows drawn together. The silky, hairless flesh of his groin and inner thighs, like his face, blushed deep red.

Eskrill's short, slender shaft lengthened and rose from the cushion. Marcellus ran his thumb over the moist tip and around the fold of foreskin. He flicked the knob with his forefinger.

A young woman in the row ahead, bored with the rhinoceros, glanced over her shoulder and saw the boy's erection. She raised her eyebrows, covered her mouth, tittered, and looked away. Her chaperone, a middle-aged matron wearing emeralds and a painted face, glanced back to see what had amused the girl. Her mouth fell open and she looked away quickly.

"Disgusting," she muttered.

Marcellus laughed. He removed his hand from the slave's shaft, but left the chiton folded back.

"He is at that age," Marcellus said. "Always hard. Well, Magnus?"

"I want him."

"What man would not? Win the fight, and you will have him. You will have them both, together. Now go, and fight well. Eskrill and I shall be watching."

Magnus left them, his mind spinning. When he reached the file of soldiers who marked the boundary of the nobles' sector, he heard from behind him a burst of laughter and screaming. He spun about and looked back.

The rhinoceros had caught the Egyptian on its horn and catapulted him into the air. The man's body had been thrown clear of the arena and lay writhing and broken astride the inner wall, bleeding in great spurts from the gaping hole in his chest. Two soldiers broke from the file, rushed down the aisle, and threw the offending body back into the arena.

The painted matron, who had been so scandalized by the sight of Eskrill's erect, denuded shaft, was clapping and shrieking with excitement, oblivious of the blood spattered across the hem of her gown.

Magnus turned and hurried on.

# – Two –

In the gladiators' quarters, Urius continued to use the Syrian. The other gladiators were still gathered around him in a circle, many now naked from the waist down and stroking their shafts. Urius stood in the center, his arms at his sides, his thick, flaccid shaft hanging outward from his groin and pointing down at Zenobius. The slaveboy lay cringing at his feet, covered with sweat and dust, sobbing.

As the men watched, Urius began to urinate. The blond gladiator grinned and rolled his hips to aim the strong yellow stream in an arc from Zenobius's face to his crotch. The urine splashed and frothed over the slave's brown flesh and muddied the ground. The odor of human waste was heavy in the air.

Magnus was able to watch, unangered and almost forgiving of Urius for his crudity. He had Eskrill—and Erskin—to occupy his thoughts. How plain Zenobius looked, compared to the German twins!

The rhinoceros was led in from the arena. Its horn glistened with dark blood. The body of the Egyptian followed.

The sweepers with their rakes trotted out onto the field. The charioteers assembled their teams in the passageway in single file. The horses stamped, blew through their cheeks, and littered the ground with dung.

The sweepers returned; the gamemaster gave the sign. The chariots paraded onto the track. The races began and ended. The time for the final match arrived.

Magnus gathered up his sword and shield; no armor would be worn in the death match.

The Nubian awaited him in the passageway. They exchanged cold stares, then entered the arena together. They marched across the field

*Slaves of the Empire*
Published by The Haworth Press, Inc., 2006. All rights reserved.
doi:10.1300/5502_02

to the Imperial box and raised their swords to the Emperor. The mob was hushed, saving their voices for the violence to follow.

The fight was brief, almost too brief. From the first clash of steel, Magnus knew that the Nubian was his. It was bad form to end a match with the first wound. He would have to toy with the Nubian. A successful fight was like the act of sex; it was best to hold back, to thrill the crowd as long as possible before the climax.

The energy passed from Magnus's groin into his arm, and through his fingers into his blade. His sword became his erection, hard and gleaming, eager to penetrate, unyielding and sensitive to every touch.

Magnus first deprived the Nubian of his shield. He caught the edge of the bronze plate on the tip of his sword, wrenched it from its owner's grasp and sent it skimming through the air. The mob awarded him with a reserved round of applause. The more experienced spectators knew now that the Nubian would die. They relaxed in their seats to observe the master's technique as Magnus began the process of paralyzing his victim. He began with a series of superficial wounds—cuts across the Nubian's left shoulder and arm, a slice across the man's taut belly that brought a thread of blood to the surface.

The Nubian, slashing awkwardly in desperation, drew blood—a glancing oblique scratch across Magnus' thigh. Magnus decided to end the game.

He penetrated the Nubian's defense and landed a deep cutting blow across the biceps of his sword arm, severing the thick muscle. The Nubian jumped back and transferred his sword clumsily to his left hand; his useless right arm, a burden now, hung limp and bleeding at his side. His left arm was the weaker; in seconds Magnus struck the sword from his grasp.

He made a lunge at the Nubian's lower chest and scored a deep wound.

The Nubian groaned and staggered back, but did not fall. Magnus approached him slowly, frowning; he was angry that the fight had not been more interesting. Knowing Marcellus, the senator might complain that the match had been a farce, and take back his reward.

Magnus raised his sword, swung it upward and down, upward and down, marking a crimson X across the Nubian's dark chest.

The mob roared. Still the Nubian did not fall. Magnus flicked the tip of his blade about the Nubian's skirt and cut the strap that held the man's leather cup. The garments fell away and the Nubian stood, naked, his arms hanging useless at his sides.

There was a hush from the mob. They were eternally curious, the sedate merchant class in particular, about the dimensions of any shaft that was not white. It was always good theater to indulge their prurience.

The Nubian's sex was swollen, almost erect; Magnus had seen this curious phenomenon before in his victims, the concentration of blood in the sex even as it drained from the rest of the body. He slid his sword between the man's legs, forcing him to open his thighs and rise to his toes. He lifted the Nubian's shaft for display, the fleshy rod lay balanced along the sharp edge of his blade.

The crowd was silent. Magnus looked at the Nubian's face. His dark eyes begged for an end to the humiliation, for release into death.

Magnus lowered the pommel of his sword and stabbed upward, entering the Nubian below his testicles and impaling him on the blade. A rain of blood and offal poured hot over Magnus's fist. A thrill like fire ran from the buried steel into Magnus' arm, welling in his chest and filling his leather codpiece.

The Nubian screamed in spastic agony. The mob roared. There were shrieks among the crowd. Hysteria filled the coliseum.

Magnus pulled his sword free and stepped back. The Nubian jerked wildly and collapsed to his knees. Magnus raised his foot to the man's throat and pushed him backward to the ground. He placed his sword to the Nubian's chest and looked to the Imperial box.

The Nubian's performance had been disastrous. There could have been no reprieve for him, even if there were a chance that he might survive his wounds. The Emperor extended his arm and made a fist, thumb pointing down.

Magnus drove his sword into the Nubian's heart. There was no thrill in the penetration. His sword was lifeless again, insensate; the power had returned to his shaft.

The Emperor and his court saluted him. The mob cheered wildly as he walked the circuit of the arena, raising the bloody sword for their adoration. The fight had been unremarkable, even mediocre, but Magnus had given them a climax that would be talked about in the bazaars and palaces and slave quarters for many days.

As he passed the nobles, Magnus searched the stands for Marcellus and the boy. His eyes found the painted matron first. She had fainted. Her head had fallen on the lap of her young charge. The ingénue seemed unaware of the weight as she bounced on her cushion and clapped. She tried frantically to catch his eye, but Magnus looked above and beyond her, at Eskrill.

The slaveboy's chiton was still folded back. Marcellus was running his fingers idly over the boy's shaft, keeping him erect. Magnus looked at Eskrill's face. The boy stared back at him, eyes wide with fright. He looked at Marcellus; the senator's expression was as flat and inscrutable as ever.

Magnus circled the arena twice. The applause grew louder. Garlands were thrown before his feet. An emissary from the Emperor crowned him with a golden wreath.

In the gladiators' quarters, the athletes hailed him in subdued tones, too in awe of him to shout. Urius stood apart, leaning against a pillar, one foot planted on the back of the Syrian slaveboy; Zenobius lay collapsed in the dust, unconscious after his long ordeal. Urius was cleaning his nails with a dagger and scarcely looked up.

An attendant rushed to take Magnus's sword and shield. The slave spoke to him in a low voice and nodded toward the entrance. "You have visitors, master."

Magnus turned and saw that Marcellus was approaching him, followed by Eskrill a few paces behind.

The senator raised his hand in greeting. "An extraordinary finish, Magnus; I have never before seen anything quite like it. Something must have inspired you."

Magnus nodded absently. He stepped past Marcellus and went to Eskrill. The red haze was upon him.

The boy saw the look in his eyes and turned his face away. He trembled and would not look up.

Magnus took the boy's chin in his hand and tilted his face up. He tightened his grip on the slave's jaw, pulled him onto his toes, and kissed him. Eskrill's hands flew to Magnus's hips, searching for balance.

From the corner of his eye, Magnus saw that Urius had drawn closer and was watching them.

Magnus moved his hand over the slave's chest, cupping his pectoral and pinching the swollen nipple between his fingernails. He caught the boy's sigh in his mouth and broke the kiss. Eskrill's eyes were tightly shut.

"I pity you, boy," Magnus murmured, breathing the words into Eskrill's face. He touched his lips to the slave's eyelids. "I pity you for the things I shall do to you."

Magnus turned his head to observe Urius's reaction. He was surprised, and disappointed, to see no sign of envy on the gladiator's face. Urius seemed more amused than jealous.

A hand fell on Magnus's shoulder. "Not yet," Marcellus said softly. "Not yet. Tonight. Both of them together."

Magnus released the boy, who backed away and lowered his eyes to the floor. Marcellus stepped between the gladiator and the slaveboy.

"Eskrill and I shall return to the villa now, to prepare for your visit. I have already spoken to Harmon; you are free for the evening. Do not bother to bathe or eat. Tonight, my home and all its comforts are yours. I will send a litter for you in an hour."

# – Three –

After the gladiators and charioteers had taken their final victory march across the arena, and the games were officially closed by the Emperor, Magnus returned to the athletes' quarters. He stripped off his fighting gear and allowed one of the attendants to sponge the Nubian's blood from his body, then to dress him in a chiton made of red silk, imported from Antioch—his best, since Marcellus was to be his host for the evening—belted high at the waist with a thick band of Spanish leather. The litter arrived within the hour, as Marcellus had said it would.

Magnus could have reached the senator's villa more quickly by horse or by chariot; but the litter was a luxury he had never experienced. He had walked or ridden beside Harmon's litter, but the merchant had never allowed him to be carried inside.

It was an unexpected pleasure—to be carried aloft, without having to consider the route or control a team of horses. The litter that Marcellus sent had a boxlike canopy hung with yellow curtains, supported by two long beams of polished oak that were in turn supported on the broad shoulders of eight slaves, four on either side. The curtains were tied back with thin silver chains; the box was strewn with soft yellow cushions that smelled of sandalwood. Among the cushions Magnus found a skin of red wine.

He settled himself among the cushions, uncorked the skin, and squeezed a spray of wine into his mouth. The wine splashed off his lips, wetting his beard and dripping invisibly onto the deep red silk of his chiton. Magnus looked around and behind, studying the slaves who carried him through the dense traffic outside the coliseum. They were alike as a team of high-bred horses: strong, dark-skinned Levantines with hairy chests, dressed in white linen loincloths and thick-

*Slaves of the Empire*
Published by The Haworth Press, Inc., 2006. All rights reserved.
doi:10.1300/5502_03

soled sandals. Like all Marcellus's slaves, they wore broad collars of gold around their burly necks.

The late afternoon was warm. Shadows were long; the moon was already showing her face in the pale blue sky, low in the east. The strangeness of the light, the unaccustomed luxury of the litter, the splashing of the red wine in his mouth and the relaxation of his body after the tension of the arena, all cast Magnus into a dreamy mood. The bearers carried him high above the heads of the citizens who thronged the inner streets of the city. Everywhere men stood in groups, drinking and loudly reminiscing about the day's events in the coliseum, lowering their voices in awe to speak of the thrilling performance given by Magnus the gladiator.

He passed a group of ploughboys in town for the game day, stretching their stocky legs and turning their tousled heads to take in all the excitement, looking for whores or city boys to show them the town. The youths saw him and shouted his name, jostling each other and waving with excitement.

Magnus waved at the boys and smiled. He would have liked to have stopped the litter bearers and taken a moment to speak with the boys. Magnus liked country boys, with their smooth complexions and strong young bodies. They were always in awe of him, eager to listen to him talk about the arena; and many of them were more than willing, after he had met them in the marketplace or baths, to return with him to his small apartment in the coliseum. It was a common dream among such boys, he had learned, to be taken to bed by the great gladiator Magnus.

The young provincials were not jaded, like city boys, or tainted, like the attendants at the coliseum. They rendered a kind of worship to his scarred limbs and rigid staff, as if each wound were a mark of his triumph over the Fates, and his sex a magnified talisman of their own beginning masculinity. The excitement of such boys, so pure and intense, was contagious. Their willingness, their eagerness to please him, even to abase themselves before him, was intoxicating.

Cruising the markets and baths on festal days or game days, Magnus had encountered many virgins. The virgin boys, and even some of the more experienced youths, were always amazed and more than a little frightened when they first laid eyes on the shaft they were expected to serve. Magnus enjoyed coaxing a virgin—instructing the boy first to hold the staff in his hands, to accustom himself to its length and girth; then to kiss it, lick it, take what he could in his mouth. Then came the moment that Magnus prized: seeing the fear on a virgin's face when the boy, having experienced the shaft with his hands and lips, contemplated the dimension of the surrender that was demanded of him. But despite the fear, not one of them had refused to obey, even if they trembled, when Magnus told them to squat above him and impale themselves on his sex.

He remembered, in particular, a boy he had met some weeks before, during the festival of Diana; a fresh young farm boy, his family ruined by debts, who had been reduced to begging in the city streets. The smudges of soot on his face and the tattered clothing he wore could not conceal the firmness of his lean body or the downy smoothness of his cheeks. Magnus had fed him bread and cheese in the marketplace; the boy had been hungry as a wolf. He bought the boy a fresh linen tunic and took him to the baths.

Afterward, his belly full, the mud and sweat washed from his flesh, dressed in white, the boy had offered his gratitude in a stammering voice and expressed his willingness, with eyes averted, to perform any duty Magnus might require of him.

The boy was a virgin, but not naive. In Magnus' rooms he began to strip, even before Magnus told him to. Later, squatting above the gladiator, impaled on the very tip of his shaft, the boy had begun to cry with frustration, certain he could take no more. Magnus had been moved by the tears, but the seduction had proceeded too far to be cut short. He clamped his strong hands onto the boy's hips and pulled him relentlessly downward. It had been an ordeal for the boy—his face became twisted with pain, he whimpered, his chest became glossy with sweat and his breathing grew ragged. With agonizing slowness, Magnus took the boy's virginity.

And when the penetration was complete, a wondrous transformation had taken place: The boy began to laugh and sob together, elated that he had proven worthy, proud that he had been able, despite himself, to accommodate the shaft, desperate to give it pleasure.

Magnus had fucked him three times that night, and when the boy's ass was too raw and aching to take him again, he had turned his attention to the boy's virgin mouth. By morning, the boy had learned to take the full length of the rod down his throat as smoothly as a temple whore. He gorged himself on Magnus's flesh, as ravenously as he had taken the bread and cheese in the marketplace. Magnus responded to his hunger, climaxing twice in the eager mouth without growing soft, filling the boy's belly with semen.

The light of noon had found both of them pale and exhausted, drained and covered with sweat. The boy's lips were puffy and swollen, his throat as sore as his ass; but there was a smile of contentment on his face. Magnus rolled him onto his belly and, against the boy's feeble protests, took him a final time. After they had bathed and eaten, Magnus had taken the boy to the Temple of Elagabalus and introduced him to the high priest. The boy would no longer have to beg for his sustenance; his mouth and his ass would support him.

Remembering the boy had caused Magnus's shaft to unfurl and lengthen beneath the skirt of his chiton. Magnus felt a sudden compulsion to be alone and naked. He unhooked the silver chains and let the curtains of the litter fall shut. The box was filled with filtered yellow light.

Magnus loosened the wide leather belt around his waist and pulled the chiton over his shoulders. He fell back into the bank of cushions and ran his hands over his chest and between his legs. He looked down at his body and flexed each muscle as he touched it. The smooth, sun-bronzed flesh seemed lit from within under the yellow glow of the curtains. The dense dark hair on his chest was touched with amber points of light.

A sense of great luxury settled over him. He could hear passing voices in the street, sense the mass of bodies all around him, just beyond the curtains, but within the box he was hidden and alone, invisible to the crowd. He closed his eyes and thought of the grateful virgin. He touched his forefinger to the base of his shaft and pointed it straight from his groin, as he had done when he had offered it for the kneeling youth to suck. He stroked himself, recalling the clutching heat of the boy's ass and the choking sounds he had made when Magnus fucked his throat.

Then Magnus remembered the twins, the slaveboys Eskrill and Erskin, who awaited him at Marcellus's villa. He drew his hand away and shook himself out of the reverie.

Magnus had often known the pedestrian's curiosity when a closed litter passed and the crowd was cheated of the sight of whatever personage moved among them. When the litter bearers paused at a crossing, waiting for a train of oxen to pass, he was seized by an impulse to reveal himself. He leaned forward, bending sharply at the waist, and parted the curtains to his right.

The litter bearer whose shoulder supported the central weight of the box, a young Levantine with a bristling moustache and large lips, glanced up at him and quickly looked away. Only one other person saw him, a matronly woman a few paces distant who stood at the edge of a covered vegetable market, waiting in the lowering sunlight while her servant girl selected the purchases. The matron was in her middle years, a handsome woman with brightly painted eyes and lips. She was dressed in a simple but expensive green robe, too tasteful for a merchant's wife; the mistress of a senator or a general, perhaps. The woman saw him and lifted her penciled eyebrows. Her eyes raked over his naked body, then focused on the staff of flesh jutting upright from his lap, curving upward like the handle of an urn to touch the hard bands of muscle beneath his pectorals. Her eyes became hot as coals. She looked up at Magnus's face. She licked her lips and seemed about to speak.

Magnus let the curtains fall shut. He fell back into the pillows, laughing softly. The litter jerked and began to move.

Magnus ran his hands over his body, touching himself everywhere, but avoiding the tower of flesh between his legs. He pressed his fingers into the soft, wiry hair around the base of his shaft, causing the rod to rise from his belly and stand up straight. He remembered the Levantine slave, and the brief glance of desire the man had given him. He rolled onto his side and parted the curtains an inch. He saw the man's long nose, bobbing up and down as he bore the beam across his shoulder and trotted.

Magnus straightened his body and pushed his shaft through the opening in the curtains. He did not have to speak. He heard a quiet gasp, and then the slave took the offered shaft into his mouth, swallowing it until his lips were pressed against the curtains, somehow managing to keep step with the other litter bearers while he sucked.

Magnus lay on his side, his head filled with the sounds of the street. The slave's mouth bathed his shaft with warmth. Magnus was hidden within the box, his sex hidden in the Levantine's throat. The movement of the slave's head as he ran provided a constant, urgent stroking.

The noise of the city gradually receded. The bearers carried him outside the city walls. Many times he came close to spilling his semen; but Magnus had no intention of wasting his seed in the Levantine's belly. At last he rolled onto his back, pulling his rod from the slave's mouth. The long, thick shaft was heavy with blood, slick with saliva. Magnus grabbed a cushion and wiped himself dry, then pulled his chiton back over his shoulders.

He opened all the curtains and felt the cool evening air rush over him. He looked at the darkling green fields, at the strong naked backs of the men who bore him, moist and glistening under the slanting light of the sun. He glanced at the Levantine below him. The man looked steadily ahead. His mouth and chin were glossy with spit; there was a faint smile on his lips.

Marcellus's villa was not far from the city, situated in the midst of vineyards at the end of a narrow, unpaved road lined with cypress trees. Magnus arrived at the last hour of the day.

The white columns of the great house were pale blue in the twilight. The ornamental pools in the courtyard reflected stars in a darkening sky. The statues of Apollo and Venus that flanked the portal seemed almost alive in the uncertain light.

Marcellus greeted him at the door. His face was flushed and his expression unusually frank and amiable. His toga was crooked, as if he had just pulled it on; his hair was moist and pushed to one side. He smelled faintly of sweat. When he spoke, Magnus caught a hint of wine on his breath.

"The litter bearers were satisfactory?" Marcellus's voice contained an insinuation of punishment.

"Yes," Magnus said. He could not resist smiling, remembering the smooth heat of the Levantine slave's mouth.

Marcellus nodded. "Good." He turned and gestured for Magnus to follow. "I've been busy, preparing for you. Eskrill had to be punished first, for his impudence at the games."

Magnus was able to guess, then, the reason for the senator's disarray. He had hoped the boy would be fresh for him; instead, Marcellus had been abusing him.

Marcellus saw his look of disappointment. "Don't worry," he said. "He hasn't been harmed, only humiliated. All the readier for you to use him."

In the foyer, two young eunuchs awaited them. The slaves were naked, the strings of blue Aegean pearls that circled their hips concealed nothing. Their bodies were well proportioned, attractively fleshy and utterly hairless; even their heads were smooth. Their small organs seemed almost incidental, incongruous stubs of flesh protruding from the downy swelling between their thighs. Only a small faded scar showed where their testicles had once been.

"You'll want to bathe before you eat," Marcellus said. "The eunuchs will attend to you."

Marcellus walked to the closest of the boys and affectionately stroked his face. "They have been with me for a long time. I bought them years ago in Alexandria, when they were only infants. The Alexandrian slave market is an extraordinary place, so much more exotic than Ostia." He played his fingers among the dangling pearls, then squeezed the boy's tiny penis between his thumb and forefinger. "If it is a eunuch you wish to buy, not a whole boy, they will perform the castration free of charge on any slave up to twelve years of age. They do it there on the auction block, for all to see."

Marcellus turned his back on the eunuch and smiled grimly at Magnus. "I'll leave you now. The slaves will see to your comfort."

Magnus was left alone with the eunuchs. They led him out of the foyer, through the sprawling corridors of the house to a wide, high atrium lit by a skylight of pink glass. They unbuckled his belt, untied his sandals, and lifted the chiton over his head. They gestured to a heated pool of fragrant water. Then the eunuchs left him.

Magnus lowered himself into the pool. The steaming water eddied about his body, relaxing the tightness of his muscles and soothing the tensions in his groin. Magnus closed his eyes and dozed.


After a time, the eunuchs returned.

They led him from the pool to a low divan. As the cool air struck his body, his muscles seemed to dissolve and a curious lightness filled his limbs and chest. His back seemed almost to hover above the padded surface of the divan.

The eunuchs knelt beside him. Gently positioning his body, they used their mouths to clean his hands and feet, and then his armpits. They ran their tongues in broad strokes over his arms and legs and together sucked the moisture from the dense mat of hair on his chest; then they converged upon his genitals. One attended to his shaft, licking and kissing it; the other mouthed his testicles and delicately stroked the moist flesh beneath with his tongue.

They carefully turned him onto his stomach and pulled his thighs apart. One of them cleaned the space between his cheeks, holding the relaxed muscles apart and licking the crevice with long strokes from the base of Magnus's testicles to the small of his back; when he was done, the other put his mouth on the opening itself, sucking at the wrinkled circle of flesh, licking at the loosened debris. Both eunuchs then took turns inserting their tongues into his ass. They lingered over the task, as if the flavor they found there excited them. Their tongues reached more and more deeply into him, stroking the slick inner walls, like kittens vying for the last morsel of nourishment in a narrow vessel.

Magnus surrendered himself to the unique sensation. When he had been no more than a slaveboy himself, rowing on Harmon's ship, the galley master had frequently used his ass; but since that time no man had entered or even touched him there. He had never felt, or imagined, the workings of a tongue inside him. The eunuchs' devotion relaxed him to a degree he had never experienced before. Even his shaft was loosened and soft.

Then he imagined that it was Eskrill's tongue burrowing deeply into his bowels, and his shaft began to harden.

After the bath, the eunuchs led him through a wooden door into a cubicle filled with steam. They stayed beside him in the swirling mist, scraping his sweating flesh with stiff bands of leather. Afterward they laid him on the divan again. They massaged each muscle of his body, beginning with his abdomen and ending with his fingers and toes.

They immersed him in a pool of cool, clear water. They dried him with soft red towels. Then, as he stood before them cleansed, relaxed, glowing with comfort, they applied a thin sheen of oil to his flesh, even to the soles of his feet and his face, so that his thighs slid against each other when he walked and his rippling back shone under the newly lit torches like a cascade of liquid gold.

They dressed him in the red chiton and the wide belt and led him barefoot across gleaming marble floors to an empty banquet hall. They knelt on cushions beside him, fed him with their hands, and lifted goblets of wine to his lips. Having nothing to do, his hands moved idly over their naked bodies, cupping the firm fleshiness of their breasts, squeezing the soft fullness of their asses, reaching through the chain of pearls to stroke the smooth, sensitive places where their testicles had been removed.

Magnus settled into the easy rhythm of luxury, awaiting the appearance of the twins without impatience. It was a splendid gift that Marcellus had given him: an evening that allowed him the fantasy of being a free man, a wealthy man, an owner of litter bearers and eunuchs and slaveboys from the North.

Magnus was intoxicated with power—the ironlike power of his sex, always present, and added to it the power, illusory but potent, of being an owner of men's bodies. Strong shoulders to bear him smoothly above the crowd, skilled hands to massage him, and moist tongues to wash the hidden places of his body; and waiting somewhere in the vast house, the perfect golden bodies of the captured barbarian princes.

Magnus had never had absolute power over another body. He had used Harmon's mouth and ass thousands of times—for months, in the beginning, he had fucked the merchant twice or three times a day. But Harmon was his owner, and even though he debased himself before Magnus's sex, there were clear limits beyond which Magnus could not go; and Harmon was old and soft.

There were the youths he found in the markets and baths. They were beautiful, but he did not own them. He could slap them, perhaps, but he could not bruise them; seduce them, but never rape them. They were free boys, with laws to protect them from abuse. A suit for damages brought to Harmon from an angry father could wreck Magnus's popularity and send him back to the galleys.

There were, of course, the attendants at the coliseum. He was free to use any of them whenever he pleased, as Urius had done that afternoon with the Syrian slave, Zenobius. Some of them were skilled enough; few boys, certainly, could swallow a shift like Zenobius, whose throat could accommodate even Urius's godlike mallet. The attendants existed to keep the athletes content. If that meant a scar across the face, a broken rib, or even death, it did not matter. The gamemaster would simply obtain another from the slave market at Ostia.

But the attendants meant little more to Magnus than vessels to be plugged with his shaft after a killing. They were uniformly attractive, but none of them extraordinary—like Eskrill. A slaveboy as beautiful as that would only be found in a rich man's bedchamber, never in the coliseum. And the attendants presented no challenge, no mystery. Most, like Zenobius, had been reduced to ciphers, without personality or resistance, living only to avoid pain and to endure the explosive assaults of the man they served.

Tonight, Magnus had been elevated above the common run of his life; he was to be the master of two proud Germanic princes, strong-willed barbarian youths who had been made to grovel under the heel of the Empire. Magnus had been intrigued by the lingering pride he had seen in Eskrill that afternoon. Marcellus claimed that he had broken the boys. They were broken, perhaps, but not shattered. Magnus had sensed a flame inside the boy, a last vestige of will that Marcellus, blinded by his egomania, could not see.

Marcellus's loan of the boys was a challenge. Magnus vowed to himself that the boys would not be unchanged by his hours with them. When Marcellus found them in the morning, they would be as naked of their masculinity, as docile and ingratiating as the two eunuchs. . . .

There was a change in the room, something indefinite and unseen that drew Magnus back to the present moment.

The eunuchs had vanished, but Magnus was not alone. Across the room, at the top of a short flight of steps, a military man with folded arms stood framed between two pillars of green marble, watching him.

Above the waist, the officer was naked except for a pectoral made of golden discs spangled across his chest and a red cape embroidered with gold, gathered at his neck by a golden clasp in the shape of an eagle. The cloth was pushed back from his shoulders, exposing muscular arms. An open bracelet in the shape of a snake—like the eagle and pectoral, made of gold—was coiled about the biceps of his right arm. The officer wore a skirt of banded leather straps slung low enough to expose his navel. The straps descended midway to his knees, leaving most of his muscular thighs bare. His shins were covered by bronze greaves laced tightly to his calves.

Magnus opened his mouth to ask the stranger's name, then drew his brows together. The man was not a stranger. It was his host.

# – Four –

The senator descended the steps and approached. The soft slapping of his sandals against the marble floor echoed through the high chamber. The long red cape billowed silently behind him. To Magnus, in his bemused state, the rhythm of Marcellus's steps and the rippling of the red folds of cloth seemed a sound and a sight remote from the ordinary, simple yet mysterious, strangely alluring.

Marcellus stood before him. Magnus looked up at him, unable to raise his eyes above the dazzling golden pectoral that adorned Marcellus's chest. The body he saw seemed to be that of a man much younger than a senator. The arms, usually concealed in the loose sleeves of a senatorial toga, were thick with muscle, more like the limbs of a smith than a noble. The legs were long and firm, dark with hair. Their massive girth suggested steadfast power, as if, like twin pillars, once set against the earth no amount of strength could move them.

The flatness of the senator's belly surprised Magnus. There was no sign of debauchery there, only the faintest layer of fat, the mark of a strong, healthy appetite, spread thin above hard clusters of scalloped muscle.

The golden pectoral Marcellus wore was made of coins. The coins were clearly of barbaric origin, roughly cut and stamped with crude profiles. Beneath the mesh of gold wire that knit the discs together, the symmetrical muscles of Marcellus's broad chest were clearly defined, covered with a mat of hair as black and finely curled as the hair on his head. His nipples were the color of copper, set like ornaments at the corner of each breast, as flat and round as the golden coins.

The body before him was like a discovered secret, its revelation another of the evening's special favors. Even at his private parties, Marcellus dressed with the decorum of his rank, in flowing robes that gave no hint of the magnificence they concealed.

*Slaves of the Empire*
Published by The Haworth Press, Inc., 2006. All rights reserved.
doi:10.1300/5502_04

To Magnus's surprise, the sight of Marcellus's body excited him. Magnus's staff had begun to harden, tenting the skirt of his chiton, and he felt a vague longing to touch himself. He glanced at the other man's hips, curious, as he had never been before, about Marcellus's sex. The leather straps lay flat across the senator's thighs, but curved outward between his legs, an intimation of something unexpectedly large beneath.

"I trust the eunuchs pleased you." Marcellus's voice, low and measured, seemed deliberately seductive.

"Yes." Magnus raised his eyes at last to the senator's face. It was the stony inflexibility there, and the touches of silver at Marcellus's temples, that had always distracted Magnus from taking notice of the man's body. Marcellus's face, after all, was not as old as Magnus had thought. He had confused authority with age.

The sternness of the senator's face and the contemptuous line of his mouth, together with the ageless strength of his body, suggested to Magnus the image of a god. Not the gods of boyhood, Mercury or Apollo; Vulcan, perhaps, or more likely Jupiter, master of order and shaper of the greater destinies. Magnus felt an unaccustomed and uncomfortable feeling of submission, seated before the standing man. To relieve it, he decided to stand, but a sudden dizziness of wine forced him back.

He found himself unable to take his eyes from Marcellus's body. He knew, as long as the senator stood before him, that he would be content to watch the rise and fall of the golden pectoral, and to study in fleeting glances the uncertain bulk beneath the leather skirt.

It was said that Marcellus, when he commanded the legions in Iberia, had been regarded by his men as semidivine. Magnus understood in that instant the source of the soldiers' devotion and faith. This was how they had seen the man, dressed not in the shapeless robes of a senator, but in martial red and gold, hard bronze and leather. They had looked up from below to see him astride his mount, his massive thighs pressed against his horse's flanks, his muscular arms naked and bearing a sword and banner.

Marcellus seemed to follow the course of his thoughts. He raised his right hand to the golden pectoral; the golden snake wrapped itself more tightly around his biceps. "This is the uniform—some of the uniform—that I wore in my final campaign. The coins are from every corner of Iberia; they show the faces of the petty tyrants who styled themselves gods, before I crushed them.

"I dress this way, sometimes, when I discipline the twins. They understand the authority of these symbols. They remember the terror of the battle in which they were taken prisoner, ringed by Roman steel. These garments remind them of what I was, a warrior; remind them of what they were and no longer are."

A wave of jealous distaste, like the anger Magnus had felt observing Urius abuse the Syrian slave, mingled with the unexpected desire Marcellus conjured in him. Magnus thought of the two eunuchs and knew that it was the body before him that they had been trained to please with their hands and mouths. He imagined Marcellus, dressed as he was, with the German twins groveling at his feet. Magnus became impatient.

"Where are the boys?" he snapped.

The muscles around Marcellus' mouth tightened, and Magnus immediately regretted his sharpness. But the hard line of Marcellus's lips curved into a smile.

"I was wondering what thoughts were causing that sudden stirring beneath your skirt. You've waited long enough. It's time for your reward. I still feel a rush of excitement when I think of how you handled the Nubian in the arena today."

Magnus rose. The lightness in his head had subsided. He followed the billowing folds of the senator's cape.

They left the banquet hall and entered a long, straight vestibule. Polycandelions, carved in the shape of griffins with squat candles in their mouths, hung from the ceiling, filling the hall with amber light. The walls were painted with murals in shades of red, dark green, and yellow, depicting scenes of warfare, worship and Bacchanalia. At intervals, family busts were set into niches in the walls. The marble faces, male and female alike, recalled Marcellus's face; all had the same broad jaw and grim, faintly smiling lips.

A door at the end of the vestibule opened into fresh air. They walked through a covered portico to a large, low annex made of stone, situated at the side of the main house. The cool evening air was filled with the soughing of crickets. The full moon was still low in the east.

Marcellus pushed upon two high wooden doors and entered the stone building. Magnus followed. The air within was warm. He felt and heard the soft crackling of straw beneath his feet. The mealy smells of millet and dung closed about him.

A single torch set into a post illuminated the stables. The shapes of horses in their stalls, standing as they slept, loomed shadowy and indistinct. The beaten surface of an anvil glinted in the wavering light. The room was filled with huge, jumping shadows and the quiet breath of the slumbering horses.

"I keep them here," Marcellus said in a low voice, "in the stables. They go nude in the daytime. They eat and drink from their own trough. They void themselves on the straw."

The senator lifted a heavy iron mallet and studied it under the torchlight. The weight caused his biceps to flex massively; the straining muscle seemed about to break the golden serpent wrapped tightly around it.

"During the day," he said, "they work. They carry burdens too heavy for the old stable master, brush the horses, shovel dung and hay. The smith is teaching them to use their arms at the forge. I do not want their bodies to ever grow soft."

Marcellus set the mallet aside, lifted a block of wood from a bolted door and pulled it open. "This is where I keep them at night. Watch your footing. The stairs are old and narrow."

Magnus followed the senator down a steep flight of granite steps worn smooth with age. There was a reddish glow from below, and rising warmth.

Marcellus continued to speak in a low voice. "The smith assists me in securing them for the night. I suspect he uses the boys himself occasionally, but as long as he leaves no signs of it, I suppose it is his due. The eunuchs help me to care for them—washing them, shaving and oiling their bodies. Except for the old stable master, they see no one else. My wife would hardly know of their existence if it were not for all the gossips among her servants."

The stairs ended. A short, low passageway led to an underground room. At first Magnus thought the chamber was immense, extending beyond the dimensions of the stable above; then he saw that the walls were made of highly polished black marble. The reflective darkness of the stone deceived the eye, creating the illusion that the room extended to infinity.

The chamber was, nevertheless, quite spacious, though the beamed ceiling was low. At the center of the room stood a huge round brazier. Smoke from the high, crackling flames pooled about the ceiling, eddied and swiftly dispersed through a grating of iron bars set at ground level along the top of one wall. The grating was blue with moonlight.

Magnus's eyes were caught by the leaping flames. He felt the heat of the brazier on his face and arms, felt beads of sweat break from his oiled flesh. He looked deeper into the fire, between and through the tongues of flame, and saw beyond them a form the color of human flesh.

Magnus heard a sound from far away, above and behind him—a heavy wooden bolt falling into place. He turned to see that Marcellus had disappeared. The senator had silently retreated up the steps, closed the door and barred it behind him.

The moment had arrived. A delicious sense of anticipation settled over him, the sweetest of all the sweet sensations he had experienced that night. Magnus stood for a long moment, studying the naked body across the room in glimpses through the flames.

He could distinguish few details—only a glimmering shape, bright in the firelight; a naked boy with a thick torso and stocky limbs, prostrated on his elbows and knees. Through a sudden break in the flames, Magnus saw distinctly the curvature of the boy's uplifted ass. The half-moon of pale flesh was silhouetted against the blackness beyond. Magnus followed the uninterrupted line with his eye as it arched upward, around and down to meet and melt into the subtler curve of his boy's well-muscled thigh.

Magnus's head grew light. Every sensation in his body became acute. He felt the blood drain into his groin and began to fill his staff. He reached beneath the hem of his chiton and gently squeezed the shaft between his thumb and fingers. The smooth flesh felt dense and resilient; the shaft hung outward and down, full of blood but not yet erect. Already the beveled edge of the crown was firm, as defined as lips compressed around the staff. Through his fingers, Magnus felt the heavy throb of thick veins pulsing just beneath the taut flesh.

He circled the brazier slowly, approaching the boy from behind. As he walked, his shaft grew fully erect. The long, thick column lifted the hem of his chiton. The red silk slid back and gathered in folds at the base where the wiry hair grew dense and black. Warm air struck his testicles. The balls moved within the sack, hung loose and heavy, sliding sensuously against the smooth inner surface of his thighs.

His mind was drained of thought; it took a long moment of staring to understand all that he saw.

The boy was bound to a low block of wood. His body was naked except for golden bracelets around the neck, ankles, and wrists. His flesh was utterly hairless; the powerful legs and arms, as well as the chest and genitals, had been shaved. The head was smoothly shaved as well, and glinted as round and naked in the firelight as the boy's buttocks.

His flesh had been covered everywhere with a heavy coating of oil—not a glimmering sheen, such as the eunuchs had applied to Magnus's body, but a great, glossy, dripping mass of oil. The heavy yellow liquid poured languidly from the boy's chin and nipples and the tip of his penis, and made his denuded flesh flash in the firelight like liquid copper.

He was bound to the block of wood by leather straps across his wrists and forearms, his calves and ankles, so that he could neither raise nor lower his torso. A wide leather belt was looped around his waist. Below his navel, the belt was hooked to a short chain grounded in the wood below. The belt pulled his waist downward so that his back was deeply arched and his ass raised high.

A length of thin leather cord had been tied very tightly around the base of his shaft; another was wound around his testicles. His genitals were so swollen that they looked as if they might burst. They hardly seemed to be part of his body; the leather cut so deeply into the flesh that the organs seemed barely to connect with the smooth, hairless plane of his groin. The unnaturally bloated shaft and the knob of his testicles, hard and round as the pommel of a saddle, were red as wine. The angry color contrasted starkly with the buttery gold of his thighs.

From the boy's uplifted ass hung a dozen strands of leather, dangling from his sphincter like a tail. Magnus reached for the strands, coiled them about his fist and tugged.

The boy threw his head back and groaned.

A surge of fresh blood pulsed through Magnus's shaft. It jerked, and the swirling heat of the room was like a tongue pressed against his testicles.

The mouth of the boy's ass, like the rest of his body, had been scraped clean of hair. Magnus stared at the tightly puckered closure of flesh which gripped the dangling leather straps.

He pulled on the strands again, curious to see what held them inside the boy.

Eskrill's head jerked upward—for it had to be Eskrill, though Magnus had not yet seen the boy's face; Eskrill whom Marcellus had punished that afternoon, not beating him after all, but humbling him, shaving his entire body as he had already shaved his genitals. Magnus had not yet located the boy's twin in the room; for the moment, all his attention was claimed by Eskrill.

The boy spoke in a choking hiss: "Yes, take it out. Please, take it out of me."

As Magnus pulled on the cords, the boy's hole expanded in a smooth clenching circle. The thing within was black and made of leather, like the strands in his fist. It was round, a perfect sphere, larger in circumference than a large man's fist.

The hole grew wider and wider. The rim was pulled inside out. The tender inner flesh of the boy's ass, moist and pink, was exposed in a perfect circle like lips around the girth of the leather ball.

The ball reached its greatest width. Magnus stared, unbelieving. The boy's opening was so dilated that he might have slipped his hand inside without touching the rim.

Eskrill's body was rigid as marble. Magnus looked up and saw that his shaven head and his shoulders had grown as scarlet as his shaft. Veins stood out on the boy's neck and skull.

Eskrill's breathing was desperate, yet he managed to speak. The thin, pleading voice was ghostly in the quiet room.

"No," he whispered. "Don't stop. The rest. Take it out of me. I beg you! Take it out of me."

Magnus pulled, and watched the mouth of flesh contract quickly as the ball passed beyond its center point.

But the hole did not close. There was more within the boy.

The ball was only the base of a shaftlike leather rod; but Magnus had never seen a man's shaft as thick as this one, or as long.

Once the ball was free, Magnus no longer had to pull. Eskrill's bowels extruded the shaft with their own slow, convulsive rhythm. The boy's body trembled wildly; he panted like a woman giving birth. The huge leather shaft oozed from his ass, more and more of it, until at last and blunt tip slid free. The opening winked shut.

Magnus raised the monstrous thing before his eyes, amazed at the size and weight of it, fascinated by its glossy black surface. He gripped the ball-like base of the shaft and rubbed its tip against Eskrill's ass.

The boy shuddered. "No!" he whimpered. His voice was desperate, stripped of all pride. He shook his head wildly. His glistening body writhed.

Magnus did not see or hear. He was aware only of the ring of Eskrill's ass, pushed inward now like gumming lips around the leather shaft. As the boy had been emptied of the massive column, so he was filled again under the unrelenting pressure of Magnus's hand.

Slowly, the shaft was swallowed by Eskrill's bowels. All was inside him except the ball. His body became rigid again. The blush had seeped from his shoulders down his back; even his buttocks were bright red.

Magnus slapped one cheek. His hand left a glowing white print. Eskrill began to shiver, as if he wept.

Magnus pushed. Slowly, to the sound of crackling flames and Eskrill's ragged breathing, the sphincter opened wide. The ball slipped inside. The circle of flesh closed. Only the dangling straps, like a tail, could still be seen. The thing was inside him again.

Magnus walked to the opposite end of the wooden block. He ran his hand over Eskrill's ass and up his back, savoring the oily drag of his fingers across the boy's perfect golden flesh.

Eskrill's head was lowered. Magnus cupped the boy's chin in his hand and lifted his face.

Magnus sucked in his breath in amazement. Even the boy's eyebrows had been shaved. Without the frame of soft golden curls, without even the brows to define his face, the slave's features assumed a strange and haunting aspect. His face was covered with oil; his lips, red as fire, dripped with it. He might have been a temple whore—except that no change in his appearance, short of mutilation, could have cheapened his beauty. Even the contours of pain—the pain he must have felt from the unnatural bulk of leather impaling his ass, the humiliation of his abasement—could not disguise that awesome, perfect beauty.

Eskrill's eyes were closed, his cheeks streaked with tears. He was quietly weeping.

Magnus knelt for a moment to look upward at the finely etched muscles of the boy's hairless, gleaming chest and at his bound shaft, still stiff and plum-red—and he saw something he had not noticed before.

Hanging from a small hook on the golden collar around Eskrill's throat, as if it were the most convenient place to keep it, was a long, thin leather crop.

Magnus stood. He pulled the chiton over his head and felt the breath of heated air on his naked body.

He scooped a handful of oil from Eskrill's back and coated his shaft. He took the crop from its place on Eskrill's collar.

Magnus pointed his shaft at the boy's glistening lips.

"Open you mouth," he said quietly. "Open it wide for me."

Eskrill sobbed, his back and shoulders shuddered, but he obeyed.

Magnus stepped forward, and thrust himself in the boy's throat.

He felt the boy gag and choke around his shaft, saw him open his eyes wide in fear. He raised the crop and thrashed the boy across his shoulders and buttocks.

He felt the boy's strangled scream, reverberating through his staff. A sudden violence overcame him. He struck the boy again, and watched the nude gleaming body twist and writhe beneath him. He struck the boy across the face with the crop and felt the blow against his own shaft, through the stretched membrane of the slave's burning cheek.

Magnus did not pace himself. He was eager to spend himself. There would be more to come, an endless bounty of seed from his testicles. The sack hung heavy as lead between his thighs, slapping the boy's smooth chin.

Magnus felt his climax approach. He fucked the boy's face more furiously, listening to his liquid, strangling cries as he swung the crop with stinging force, bending forward to bury himself completely in Eskrill's throat and to slash the leather across the slave's smooth, muscled thighs.

Eskrill's face was wet with spit and oil, as red as the bloated shaft that pumped his face. Before Magnus would allow the boy to breathe again, he would fill his belly with semen.

Then, the madness gone for a time, he would pause to decide what he would do with the boy next.

# – Five –

Magnus slowly pulled his shaft from the slave's mouth. It seemed to ooze from the circling red lips, as the black leather shaft had oozed from the mouth of his ass.

Magnus narrowed his eyes at the waves of pleasure that still flowed through his groin. He looked down at his sex. The bloated shaft glistened wetly with the boy's saliva, as hard as before, jerking slightly in the aftermath of his orgasm. A bead of liquid opal gathered at the tip, then dropped and hung suspended.

Magnus took the base of the shaft in his hand and smeared the fluid across Eskrill's face, tracing the circle of his lips with the tip of his penis. The slave's mouth hung open as if the savage pounding had unhinged his jaw. His eyes were closed. His eyelids flickered, as if he were asleep and dreaming. Magnus drew back his cock and slapped with boy's face with it. Eskrill gave a start and whimpered.

The boy's beauty, even when contorted, was astounding.

Magnus's eyes roamed over the slave's shaven head, over the golden choker that circled his neck, down the wide muscles of his shoulders and back. His gaze stopped at the high, round globes of Eskrill's ass. The hard, oiled flesh, pale and smooth as porcelain when he began, was now scored with welts.

Magnus looked at the stiff leather crop in his hand. He was hardly able to remember the fury that had overwhelmed him. The marks of pain on the boy's flesh excited and disturbed him.

He walked to the slave's rear, dragging his fingers through the thick coating of oil that blurred the contours of Eskrill's back. The muscles, knotted with pain, shivered at his touch.

Magnus traced his fingertips on the welted ass. Eskrill hissed in response. Magnus tugged sharply at the tail of leather straps.

*Slaves of the Empire*
Published by The Haworth Press, Inc., 2006. All rights reserved.
doi:10.1300/5502_05

Unthinking, mesmerized, Magnus lifted the crop and let it fall with a light slap across the beaten flesh. Eskrill made no sound, but all through his body muscles tightened; the tendons of his neck drew taut, his limbs and back became like stone, his bound hands and feet curled into claws. Magnus had never seen such obscene beauty. Punishing the boy, if only to witness this sight, could become an addiction.

"Are all Romans monsters?"

The quiet, heavily accented voice intruded into the low backdrop of noise from the flaming brazier. Magnus turned slowly, surprised but not alarmed. The stupor of sex and wine had, for a time, driven the second slave, the twin, from his mind. The boy was somewhere in the room after all.

Standing so near the flames, his eyes dazzled by the reflection of the fire as it danced across Eskrill's naked and oiled body, Magnus at first could see nothing in the surrounding darkness. Then the dimness lightened by degrees, and the first thing Magnus was able to discern was his own reflection in the polished black marble of the nearest wall.

The gladiator saw himself: a tall and powerful man, naked, his staff erect, a leather crop dangling from his fist. He saw the shimmering prostrate body below him: hairless and glistening, unspeakably beautiful, subdued by bindings of hide and yellow gold.

"He is not a thing. He is a man. He was a prince. After all the madman has done to him, he is still a man."

The youthful voice called Magnus away from his own reflection. The gloom had lifted from the cellar. He could even make out the subtle shadows cast by the moonlight from the grill that ran high across one wall and opened onto the grazing area of the stables above. The shadows of the close-set bars and the cropped blades of glass between were cast, grotesquely magnified, across the stone floor.

The second slave sat huddled against one wall, his body spangled by moonlight and shadows.

He was naked and bound, like his brother, but his body had not been shaved. The light dusting of hair across his sculptured chest and limbs shown bright gold, like the bracelets around his wrists and ankles and throat.

Magnus approached the boy. As he walked, he absently tapped the crop against the calf of his leg.

The slave was blindfolded by a strap of leather wrapped tight around his head. Nevertheless, he turned his face upward at the sound of Magnus's approach.

"So you are the other one," Magnus said. "The one called Erskin."

The boy's arms were chained behind his back. His ankles were lashed together. His genitals, like his brother's, were swollen and red, tightly tied at the base with a narrow strip of hide.

His body was identical—the same stocky but gracefully shaped limbs, the broad, square shoulders, the exaggerated pectorals like slabs of polished marble. He sat with his back against the wall and his legs outstretched. The folds of flesh across his belly were tucked into flat bands, like cords of steel beneath velvet.

Yet he looked nothing like his brother. Even bound and blindfolded, he was clearly a young man taken in battle, a warrior-prince from the North. The angry set of his jaw and the tense line of his shoulders were proud and defiant. His owner had not tampered with the boy's perfection. Erskin's flesh, unshaven and unoiled, shone with its own natural silkiness. Eddies of golden hair gave a masculine frame to the smooth swellings of his chest.

Magnus pulled the leather band from the boy's head. Erskin looked up at him coldly. His dark blue eyes were luminous and wild, his pupils huge after the darkness of the blindfold. Magnus sucked in his breath. What games the Senator Marcellus played with his slaves! This was Eskrill's face, as Magnus had seen it that afternoon at the games, before Marcellus had shaved the slave's head and eyebrows. Magnus looked back at the boy, bound on his elbows and knees on the wooden block.

The resemblance between the twins was striking, but at that moment one would never have taken them to be of the same blood— hardly of the same species or sex. Erskin was a beautiful young prince, stripped and bound. Eskrill had been made into something else altogether—an object of moist openings and slick, warm surfaces, a thing to be prodded, beaten, penetrated. There was something both electrifying and sexless in his appearance, as if he were not a man at all, but a creature forged from molten glass, brought into the world more naked than mortals. His mouth and ass, his nipples and sex has been magnified by the removal of his hair.

He was a slave, not a man; a piece of property whose use was obvious. Eskrill was what his owner had made him. He was Marcellus' creation.

"You are all monsters," Erskin whispered hoarsely. The young slave still stared at Magnus, insolent and proud.

The boy's words flattened Magnus's lust. They touched a chord of guilt in him. He resented the guilt; but the boy, so serious and so handsome, pleased him nevertheless. Erskin seemed to radiate wholeness and strength—and it was the freshness and health of young men, after all, that Magnus found most attractive, even more than the exotic, pain-wracked object that Marcellus had made of Eskrill.

Magnus smiled. "You seem to know considerably more Latin than your master led me to believe."

"I listen well," Erskin said, "and I learn well. What would the madman know? He beats us if he hears us speak. So we never speak before him, and he thinks us dumb."

Magnus reached down to touch the boy's face. Erskin flinched, as if he expected to be slapped. His eyes remained wary, but when he felt the gentleness of Magnus's caress, his features softened.

Erskin lowered his face. "Are you done with him?" he said softly. "Have you finished with my brother? Release him and let him rest. He has been given too much cruelty today. Release him and use me, if you have not had enough already."

Magnus was touched by the boy's words. He saw, all at once and together, many things in the boy: devotion, bravery, and the stern resignation to Fate for which the Northern races were well known.

He stroked the boy's cheek, smooth as burnished silk. Erskin pressed his face against the callused hand in response. He trembled.

Magnus cupped the boy's chin in his hand and turned his face up. Erskin's eyes were moist. He bit his lip, as if the pain could stop the unwanted tears.

"Is it as awful as that?" Magnus asked.

Erskin caught a sob in his throat. "You cannot imagine it."

Magnus looked over his shoulder, at the boy's twin. "I can," he said.

He knelt, hooked his hands under Erskin's arms, and pulled him to his feet.

The boy was short; his face came only to Magnus's chest. Magnus circled his arms around the boy, not intending to embrace him, only to find and loosen the bindings on Erskin's wrists. But the boy seemed eager to be held. He pressed his cheek against Magnus's chest, nestling his face in the mat of dark, soft hair.

Magnus tightened his hold. The boy slowly moved his hips, rubbing himself against Magnus's chest, nestling his face in the mat of dark, soft hair, rubbing himself against the gladiator's erection.

"The chains around your wrists are locked," Magnus said softly, touching his lips to the boy's forehead.

Erskin looked up at him. His features were no longer agitated. He seemed, at the same time, somber and excited.

"Look on the table, in the corner."

Magnus glanced to his left. The table was a broad slab of black marble atop four brass legs. The surface was crowded with objects, indistinct in the firelight.

He left the boy and crossed the room. The table held bowls of fruit, bread, cheese, skins of wine, bowls of oil, implements of leather, wood, and metal. Inside a coil of thin rope, he found a ring of keys.

He released Eskrill first. The boy was stupefied, unable to speak. Magnus carried him to a bed of cushions and furs piled high beside the table. He almost dropped the burden; the slave's body was slippery with oil, and heavier than Magnus had thought, weighted with muscle. The twins were short, but their bodies were massively compact.

Magnus deposited the boy on his stomach. Eskrill hid his face in the pillows, stretched out his arms and legs and shuddered. Magnus turned him onto his side. The boy whimpered, fearing he would be forced to lie with his beaten ass against the cloth. He watched with half-open eyes as Magnus untied the bindings around his genitals and moaned with relief when he was freed.

Magnus rolled him back onto his stomach and removed the tail from his ass. He was once again excited by the slave's writhings as the enormous shaft was removed from his bowels; but Magnus restrained himself, and when the head of the man-made shaft slid free, he threw it aside.

Then Magnus crossed the room and removed the bindings from Erskin's ankles and wrists and the strap from around his sex. The boy rubbed his hands over the chafed skin around his shaft, then turned his eyes to the table.

Magnus saw that it was not the implements of torture that the boy stared at, but the food.

"When did you last eat?"

"Midday. A bowl of crushed millet and watered milk."

Magnus shook his head in disgust. "Marcellus is a fool. You will waste away on such food. Your skin will turn pasty and spotted as a beggarboy's. Go ahead. I think I saw some dried beef among the loaves of bread."

There was only one chair beside the table. Magnus allowed the boy to take it, and leaned against the table with folded arms to watch him eat.

The boy was priceless. Marcellus might have taught him obedience, but not table manners. He ate like a little barbarian, stuffing the food into his mouth and licking his lips loudly.

The fire had passed out of Magnus's blood. He was sober again, and the red haze had lifted from him. After a time, he placed his hand over the boy's grasping fist and took the half-eaten apple from his mouth. "Not so much at once," he warned. "You'll make yourself ill."

Erskin nodded. His eyelids were heavy.

"You're sleepy," Magnus said.

The slave nodded again and closed his eyes.

Magnus placed his hand on the boy's shoulder. Erskin flinched, as if he still expected some betrayal. Magnus ran his hand soothingly over the boy's collarbone and down his chest. He cupped the boy's pectoral in his hand and sighed. The muscles of Erskin's chest were solid as granite, but the flesh around his nipples was soft. The nipples were

large, smooth, and pointed. Magnus squeezed the dark circle of flesh
and pulled on it, as if he were milking it.

"Now you will use me," Erskin said. His voice was flat and bitter.

Magnus rolled the nipple between his fingers, than released it with
regret. "No," he said. "Now you will sleep."

Magnus stepped back and motioned to the bed. Erskin looked up
at him, still uncertain, then rose from the chair. He went to his
brother and knelt beside him. He ran his hands over Erskin's back,
touched the welts on his ass, and winced in sympathy. Then he lay
down beside his brother and held the sleeping boy in his arms.

Their beauty, combined, was immeasurable. Magnus settled himself close by among the furs, not touching the boys, content merely to
watch them and lazily stroke his shaft.

He thought that Erskin had fallen asleep, when the boy spoke. His
lips were pressed against his brother's shaven skull. His words were a
murmur.

"You are not a monster," he said.

Magnus rose onto one elbow, leaned forward, and kissed the boy's
ear. He looked at the two of them for a long moment, then rolled onto
his back. He soon joined them in sleep, his unspent shaft still nestled
softly in his fist.


Later, after the moon had passed her zenith and no longer cast blue
light into the cellar, and the brazier burned low, so that the chamber
was more full of shadows than light, Magnus awoke.

Erskin was pressed against him, holding Magnus's erection between his thighs. His hand slid slowly over the gladiator's arm, his fingers counting the battle scars. The boy's erection was pressed against
the lean, scalloped ridges of Magnus's belly.

The boy sensed that he was awake and looked up into his eyes.

They made love very slowly and gently, their bodies in complete
accord. Magnus held the boy's shaft while Erskin sucked him, swallowing and regurgitating the whole mass of Magnus's staff. The boy
sensed the moment when Magnus reached the brink of his climax,

and let the long, fat mallet of flesh slide free of his throat and mouth. He straddled Magnus's hips and sat on his shaft.

Magnus took the boy on his back, with his legs in the air; on his belly and his ass raised high; standing up, with his hands pressed on the floor. Erskin knelt before him and took the shaft in his mouth again. The boy's skill took him by surprise and Magnus came in his throat, long before he might have. An instant later, he felt the boy's warm semen sprayed upon his feet.

Afterward, they lay apart on the bed and talked. Erskin had not seen the games in the coliseum that afternoon, but his brother had told him of them.

"And what did Eskrill say about me?" Magnus asked.

"When he first saw you—when Marcellus sent him to fetch you from the gladiators quarters—you frightened him. Later, when he saw you fight, you frightened him more. But he said that it might not be so terrible tonight. He said that when you smiled you were not so frightening, and that he thought he saw something good in you."

Erskin asked him about his life in the coliseum, and Magnus was happy, as always when he was with a young man, to tell him about his victories and to explain the origin of each scar on his body.

He showed him the first wound he had received in the arena, a thin finger-long scar along the inside of his right thigh. Erskin ran his fingers over the faint mark, then up to Magnus's groin. He solemnly kissed the head of his staff and pressed his cheek against the big, soft mass of Magnus's testicles.

"It is so good," he whispered, "to feel a man inside me again, and to be able to like it."

Magnus ran his fingers through the boy's hair. "You hate it with Marcellus?"

"Yes." Magnus felt the slave's face blush hot against his sack. "Most of the time."

"But Marcellus is the only man you have known. He told me you were both virgins when Silvius delivered you."

"No." Erskin's voice became sharp and bitter. "I told you that Marcellus knows nothing. He imagines a thing, and the thing is real for him. Eskrill and I have never had a woman, that is true. Or any other man, before Marcellus . . . except for each other."

Magnus looked at Erskin, then at his twin, still sleeping only an arm's length away. He imagined their childhood in the North, princes raised in the same household, apart from other boys, sleeping in the same bed. Each must have been the most beautiful thing by far that the other had ever seen.

"That is one of his punishments for us," Erskin said. "That we may never touch each other. I miss it, feeling Eskrill in me, feeling myself in him." He squeezed Magnus's staff and studied it in the firelight. "We are so small, and you are so big. Are all Romans so big?"

Magnus laughed aloud and shook his head. "And what is Marcellus like?" he asked, suddenly no longer amused.

Erskin's face darkened. "Perhaps you would not like it if I told you."

"Tell me," Magnus said. He laughed slightly, to disguise the jealousy he felt. "You mean he is bigger?"

"Yes."

Magnus tried to keep the disappointment from his voice. "So much that you can tell it?"

"Magnus, you are like a god between the legs." The boy had become wary again. His fawning, born of fear, made Magnus ashamed. He lowered his voice, so that Erskin might not hear his irritation. "And Marcellus?"

"He is a monster. He is unnatural. He makes us bleed with it sometimes. He strangles us with half the length. He is like a horse. Really like a horse. One time . . ."

The boy blushed scarlet and hid his face against Magnus's thighs.

"Go on," Magnus said, unable to keep the sternness from his voice.

"One time, he took me up to the stables . . ."

"Go on."

"To the stallion he calls Rex. He made me stroke the horse's shaft until it was erect—to see if I could tell the difference, he said. Then he made me—"

Magnus stared at the beamed ceiling, imagining the scene in the stables above, horrified and excited. "Go on," he groaned.

"Please, don't make me tell the rest," Erskin whispered. "Believe me, you are better by far than Marcellus. When you are in me, there is something perfect and warm. With him there is only pain. It is the same, with the other that he brings here to use us."

"The other? Who do you mean?" Magnus's flesh grew hot.

"You must know him. He is a gladiator, like you. Marcellus has brought him here many times. Very tall, blond. Very cruel. The two of them are just alike."

A chill passed through Magnus's chest. "Urius," he whispered.

"Yes, that is what Marcellus calls him. Please, I don't want to talk of them anymore. Look—your staff has grown soft. I did not mean to—"

"And yours has grown hard," Magnus growled, looking down between the boy's thighs. "It excites you, remembering it. Urius excites you."

"I hate him," Erskin said. His voice was as cold as Magnus's. Then he looked up and blanched beneath the gladiator's anger. His body, accustomed to blows, stiffened.

Magnus saw the slave's fear, and relented. He touched Erskin's face to reassure him. The boy relaxed slowly, but his eyes were still wary.

"Believe me, Magnus, you are the first man, other than my brother, for whom I would gladly do this." He took the gladiator's shaft in his mouth and nursed at it.

Magnus lay stiffly, not touching the boy. As his staff filled with blood, a wave of cold fury eddied through him. He had been bested—not only by Marcellus, but by the man he hated most in the world. He could not bear it. He pulled the boy's head into his groin and listened to him choke. In a flash, he saw the way to drain the madness in him: to wrench the boy's face from his shaft and strike him, to strap him to the block and fill him with pain. To do what he had promised himself to do only a few hours before.

But a distant part of his mind, far from the madness radiating from his groin, saw the deeper victory already scored. He had won the boy's trust, and perhaps more than that. The anger and jealousy receded.

The tension left his limbs. He breathed deeply, and seemed to feel his whole mass swallowed and held fast in the soothing heat of Erskin's throat.

Not long after, Eskrill awoke, and by degrees joined in their love-making.

Magnus withdrew for a time, and simply watched. The twins' hunger for each other made his head go light. He watched as their bodies entwined, slid over one another, shuddered in ecstatic rhythms.

The three of them rested, ate, filled their bellies with wine, clustered together on the bed with their faces close and talked in whispers. They dozed and awoke, made love again, and slept.

Once, in the gathering darkness—for the fire in the brazier had died from neglect—Magnus heard a noise from the grating above. He looked up and thought he glimpsed four points of light, like eyes reflecting the glow of the fading coals. Then they vanished without a sound.

They might have been wolves, or sheep, sniffing at the bars. Magnus was uncertain if he had seen them at all.

# – Six –

Magnus awoke and knew instantly that he was alone.

His chest and legs were warmed by a beam of sunlight from the grating above. He looked down lazily at his body, striped by the shadows of the iron bars, and at his shaft, which lay swollen and heavy across his belly. He had dreamed of the twins while he slept, and the dreams had been as vivid as the reality of their bodies coiled around him.

He rose, stretched, paused at the table to eat a handful of grapes. He spat the seeds into the heap of gray ash that was all that remained of last night's fire.

He found his chiton where he had discarded it upon the floor, and pulled the clinging red silk over his shoulders. He looked about the cellar a final time—at the block of wood where he had beaten Eskrill, the pile of cushions and furs where he had lain with the boys, at the various objects on the table that had gone unused.

He breathed deeply, and filled his nostrils with the smells of sex, sweat, and oil. Then he mounted the narrow stone stairway that led to the stables above.

The heavy wooden door was open but not untended. One of the young eunuchs who had bathed him the night before sat beside the doorway, and hurriedly rose to his feet at the sound of Magnus's heavy footsteps.

"You slept well," the eunuch said, dusting straw from the long, sleeveless robe he wore. "I have been waiting for hours. It is almost midday."

"And where are the twins?"

The eunuch shrugged. "My lord came for them early this morning, not long after sunrise. I suppose they are somewhere in the house."

*Slaves of the Empire*
Published by The Haworth Press, Inc., 2006. All rights reserved.
doi:10.1300/5502_06

Magnus was relieved. He had thought that the boys might have risen early, found the door unbarred, and attempted to escape. It would have been insanity. With great luck and greater cunning, a slave in the outer provinces might hope to escape his master, but here, so close to Rome, escape was impossible—and the punishment harsh.

The eunuch touched Magnus's arm. His thin white fingers looked frail against the broad muscle. "My lord said he wished to see you before you left for the city. He will be in the atrium now. I will show you the way."

Magnus followed the slave out of the stable, through the covered portico and into the great house. It was good that he had the boy to guide him; within the walls he was lost, though he had walked the same hallways only hours before. The wine and anticipation had kept him from taking note of the passageways, and the house was even more enormous than he had thought.

The Senator Marcellus was in the atrium, sitting naked on the edge of the warm bath. The other eunuch was in the pool, massaging the senator's feet and legs beneath the water. A thick white towel was draped across Marcellus's loins.

Again, as it had the night before, the strength and rugged beauty of the man's body surprised Magnus. The handsome grimness of Marcellus's face unnerved him. Magnus dropped his eyes, despite himself, to the towel that concealed Marcellus's sex. The outline beneath the cloth was unclear but not uncertain. Erskin had told the truth.

Magnus hoped the interview would be brief. He did not trust himself to hold his temper.

"Join me," Marcellus said, indicating the edge of the pool to his right. Magnus sat on the tiles and let his legs sink into the water. The eunuch who had accompanied him stripped and joined his fellow in the water, and set about massaging Magnus's calves.

Marcellus leaned back on his elbows and lifted his face to the warmth that streamed from the skylight above. Magnus looked at the man's hard, muscled chest and taut belly, and again at the mound concealed beneath the towel. Something shifted under the cloth, and·

the head of Marcellus's shaft appeared between his thighs. It was dark and smooth as glass, helmet-shaped and as thick as the man's wrist.

Magnus sucked in his breath and looked away, into the water below him where the eunuch was kneading his feet with skillful fingers.

"So," Marcellus said, "you have had the twins." He turned his face to Magnus and flashed a condescending smile. "And were they as exciting as you hoped?"

Magnus cleared his throat, growing more uncomfortable with each word the senator spoke. He felt himself pulled between anger and desire and wanted only to leave. Or better, to be with Erskin again.

"I suppose," he said.

"You sound doubtful. Were they a disappointment? I cannot imagine a more docile—or more beautiful—pair of partners. If they displeased you I shall punish them."

"They pleased me very much." Magnus lowered his eyes.

"Would you like one of them for your own?"

Magnus looked at Marcellus and saw that the senator was watching his reaction closely. He tried to rid his face of expression, not wanting Marcellus to see how deeply the casual offer affected him.

"A gift, Senator?"

"Not exactly." Marcellus sat upright. The exposed fraction of his shaft withdrew from sight beneath the towel. Magnus felt a twinge of regret.

"Yesterday, Magnus, we made a bargain. You would defeat the Nubian, and I would allow you a night with the slaves. Each of us lived up to the agreement, and each of us is a happier man this morning. No?"

Magnus nodded and tried to tear his eyes from the constant, subtle motions beneath Marcellus' towel. He could have sworn that the man was flexing his shaft under the cloth, growing larger.

"Today I have another proposition for you. Much more important, involving much greater stakes. I don't expect an immediate answer. It is something you will have to consider very carefully. Have you been told whom you will be fighting in the coliseum on the next feast day? Of course not. The games are ten days away, and the matches have

not been announced. But I happen to know that you have been scheduled to fight. . . ."

"Yes?" Magnus knitted his brows; Marcellus smiled gravely at the
gladiator's suspense.

"Think, Magnus. It has been a long time coming. You are each
itching to kill the other." The senator's thin, dry laugh grated on
Magnus's nerves. "The only reason you have not fought each other before now is that you are both so valuable. It would be a shame to lose
either of you. And, of course, the gamemaster wished to wait until
the expectations of the mob reached their peak. Yesterday you both
gave extraordinary performances. The time is right. When you meet
in the arena ten days from now, the wagering will be very, very
heavy."

"Urius." Magnus whispered the name.

"Yes. The young blond god meets the dark, invincible titan. They
will be storming the gates of the coliseum to see it. The merchants
and beggars alike will wager their last denarii—and most of them will
wager on you. Urius is a superb fighter, but the oddsmakers will give
the edge to you. Therefore, I will wager on Urius. And Urius will
win."

"What? A death match? You expect me to die to line your purse?"

"No one will die. The mobs would riot if either of you were killed.
No, I have spoken to the Emperor on this matter, and he agrees. No
matter how the fight goes, the verdict will be thumbs-up. The loser
will continue his career at the coliseum. And sooner or later, no doubt,
there will be a rematch, and a chance for revenge."

Magnus shook his head in disbelief.

"Don't decide now, Magnus. It will be bitter gall, I know, to lose to
Urius. But consider: you will have the twin of your choice to soothe
you in defeat."

"How? I am a slave myself. A slave cannot own a slave."

"You will no longer be a slave. The slave shall only be a gift, to cele-
brate your freedom. That is what I am offering: to buy you your freedom."

"What you ask is impossible." Magnus kicked the eunuch aside and
pulled his legs from the water. He glared down at Marcellus.

The senator spoke in a voice that might have cut steel. "Both boys, then, for your own. Think of the favor you would be doing them, if not the pleasure for yourself. It is only a single fight, Magnus. And it will mean your freedom."

"I will leave now, Senator. I will need a horse for the ride to the City."

"Of course." Marcellus's eyes were like flame. Then he smiled his grim smile. "Tell the old stable master to give you my favorite, the stallion I call Rex."

Magnus's blood turned to ice. He turned his back on the senator and walked to the door, trembling with anger.

"Wait." Marcellus's voice was velvet again, conciliatory and relaxed. "Let the slave dry himself and show you the way."

"I will find it myself." Magnus said curtly. He paused in the doorway and turned to glare at Marcellus; but the man was no longer looking at him. He looked, instead, at the slave in the water. He crooked his finger and pointed to the towel across his loins. The eunuch obediently pulled the cloth aside, and for an instant Magnus glimpsed the monstrous shaft before it was hidden in the boy's throat.

Magnus hurried from the room.

He was blinded by fury and confusion. Soon he was lost among the spiraling chambers and endless hallways. At last he found a corridor that led to daylight, and emerged into a wooded garden behind the stables.

He paused beneath a tree for a moment to collect his senses. Then he heard a familiar, barking laugh beyond a hedge to his left. Magnus silently parted the foliage. Beyond was a clearing carpeted with grass where Urius stood naked, bathed in bright sunlight.

Urius stood still; unnaturally still, as if striking a pose. His massive legs were planted far apart, his arms relaxed at his sides. His long blond mane shone like golden silk in the light. His pale chest was dazzling, like carved crystal. His shaft, as always, was long and heavy, curving outward and down from his hips.

Magnus turned his head to see what caused the gladiator's laughter.

A few paces away, facing Urius, was a statue of white marble that mirrored his image in every detail; and kneeling beside the statue, a young Greek artisan in a chiton. The sculptor looked hardly old enough to be a master's apprentice. His hair was dark and curly. Scattered beside him on the grass was an assortment of chisels and files.

The young artist was a genius, or else his love of his subject had overcome his limitations. The statue captured the cast of Urius's body perfectly: the arrogant stance, the cruel, handsome face.

The sculptor had abandoned the conventions of modesty and duplicated the true dimensions of Urius's shaft. At that moment, he was honing the marble phallus with a small file and a polishing cloth. Urius was depicted in his usual state, half-erect. The replica had been executed with a lover's eye for detail, even to the veins that ran down its length.

The young Greek looked from Urius's shaft to the marble shaft. His face was tense with concentration.

Urius stepped closer. His staff began to thicken; it slapped against his thighs as he walked and rose in their air until the flesh dwarfed the stone.

Urius stepped even closer and crossed his arms across his broad chest. The sculptor clutched the tools in his hands and stared at the massive column of flesh. He swallowed nervously and looked up at Urius. "Let me," he whispered.

Urius shook his head gravely and raised his eyebrows, "You have asked me before, Asklepion. You know the answer: No."

"But the statue is almost done. Perhaps I will not see you again." He looked up at Urius imploringly. The gladiator was silent.

The young Greek returned his eyes to Urius's shaft. The column of flesh jerked. The young man shivered. He dropped his tools. His mouth fell open. He leaned forward and kissed the tip of Urius's rod.

The blond gladiator slapped his face away. He laughed, and began to spank the upturned, open mouth with his shaft.

Magnus withdrew in silence and hurried to the stables. He wished again that Erskin was at his side.

A few moments later, Marcellus, naked, with the white towel across his shoulder, entered the clearing in the garden.

Urius stood beside the statue, smiling broadly. Asklepion was at his feet, naked. His clothing lay in tatters on the lawn.

The young Greek was crouching between the legs of the statue. His buttocks rested on his heels; his knees were open wide. He was pulling furiously on his own shaft with both hands.

His chest was thrust forward. His head was wrenched back by Urius's fist in his hair. His eyes were open wide, gazing upward at the chiseled torso of the statue. His lips were wrapped around the long, curving shaft of marble. He masturbated wildly while Urius held him in place and forced him to suck the thick marble phallus.

The Greek's eyes rolled back, and he caught a glimpse of Marcellus. He frantically tore himself free of the fist in his hair and splayed his body low on the ground to escape the shaft in his mouth. He snatched his clothing from the grass and ran stumbling toward the house.

Urius threw his head back, laughing.

"I see the statue is almost done," Marcellus said dryly.

"The little Greek has been begging to suck my shaft since he first began," Urius said. "I told him he would have to settle for the copy, or for nothing."

Marcellus walked to the statue and ran his hands over the sleek design. "Captured forever," he sighed. "He has done well by you. Perhaps you should reward him with something more substantial than this." He took the marble phallus in his hand. The stone was warm and slick where the Greek's mouth had been.

"Why, when you let me use the twins? You're paying him well enough." Urius took the towel from Marcellus's shoulder and mopped the sweat from his forehead and arms. "So. Is that pig Magnus gone yet?"

"Yes."

"Did he take the bait?"

"No."

"I told you he wouldn't."

Marcellus shrugged. "I wanted him to choose his fate of his own free will. Perhaps he will still accept the offer. But it appears we shall have to resort to outright crime."

"In the end it will be the same," Urius said. He tossed the towel aside and squeezed his shaft. "The little Greek is a fool to think I would so much as allow him to breathe upon this beauty. When will the twins be ready for me?"

"Let them have an hour more to rest. Magnus certainly didn't exhaust them. I thought his performance last night was pathetic. Which will you want?"

Urius cocked his head and considered. "Eskrill. The shaven one. Bring him to me with the tail between his legs and his arms bound behind his back. I want to see him there, kneeling before my statue with the cold, hard marble stuffed down his throat while I punish his little cock. The hairless boy and the hairless statue."

Marcellus's breath quickened at the idea. His disappointment with Magnus was forgotten for the moment. He reached up and ran his fingers through Urius's long, golden hair, and smiled grimly.

# PART TWO

# – Seven –

For nine days following his night at the house of Marcellus, Magnus confined himself to the coliseum.

At night he slept alone in the small apartment rented for him by his owner, the merchant Harmon. During the day he trained furiously in the arena, preparing for his match with Urius.

He dreaded meeting Urius in the gladiators' quarters, uncertain whether he could contain his hatred. But he did not see Urius; the blond gladiator, according to one of the attendants, was in private training in the countryside, at the estate of a wealthy senator. Magnus had no need to ask who the senator was.

He was puzzled by the relationship between Urius and Marcellus. For how long had Marcellus been the gladiator's secret patron? How many times had Urius been invited to the senator's country villa and been allowed to use the German slaveboys?

Magnus was most puzzled by the offer Marcellus had made to him: to buy his freedom and to give him the German twins—if he would lose the match with Urius.

The senator's generosity made no sense. Did a victory for Urius mean so much to him? Magnus could not believe that the two men were lovers; they were too much alike. He could imagine neither submitting to the other, or to any man. What was the nature of the bond between them—and what did they want from him?

At night, Magnus tried not to think of the twins. He failed. If Marcellus had not given them to him for a night, Magnus would still have desired them, but no more than he desired any handsome youth. Having had them, he wanted them desperately. Having seen how they suffered in Marcellus's hands, he desperately desired to free them.

*Slaves of the Empire*
Published by The Haworth Press, Inc., 2006. All rights reserved.
doi:10.1300/5502_07

It was in his power to do so. He had only to give the fight to Urius. He himself would be made a free man—so Marcellus had promised.

The price of that freedom disgusted him. His pride was too strong and his hatred for Urius too great. Yet each night he faced the temptation to submit to the senator's bribe. As he lay alone on his pallet, he would imagine Eskrill and Erskin beside him, warm, pliant, naked— and he would feel a hollow ache in his loins.

In his loneliness, he would summon one of the attendants from the gladiators' quarters. It did not matter which. Magnus simply wished for a mouth to take his shaft while he lay unmoving on the bed, his eyes closed, his mind filled with memories of his night in the cellar of Marcellus's stables, when the German twins had been his.

Sometimes, against his will, his thoughts strayed to other images of that night and of the morning after: the sight of Marcellus in his general's garb, the awesome strength of the man's body, the unholy dimensions of his sex. Erskin had told him that Marcellus was like a horse between the legs. Magnus had glimpsed the senator's shaft only for an instant, but a glance was all that was needed for him to know that Erskin did not exaggerate.

Each night, though he fought to control his fantasies, it was not Erskin or Eskrill that Magnus saw in his mind at the instant he emptied himself into the anonymous attendant's throat. It was Marcellus he thought of, as his orgasm approached and overwhelmed him: Marcellus's cruel, flashing eyes and powerful jaw, his massive limbs and broad chest, his godlike shaft. Helplessly, Magnus imagined that shaft thrust like a sword down his throat, wrenching his jaws apart. He imagined it inside him, his bowels impaled on its impossible length.

When at last he had spent himself in the attendant's mouth, he was freed from these irresistible and hateful imaginings. Magnus would send the slave away so that he could be alone with his misery and confusion.

He would pray then to Morpheus, the god of sleep; and though the divinity took his time in answering Magnus's plea, and the candles burned low, eventually Magnus would be granted the release into oblivion that he sought.

During the day, he emptied his mind by taxing his body. He ran the circuit of the arena over and over, strengthening the stamina of his legs and lungs. He practiced each weapon with the best of the training masters, and when one partner was exhausted, he called for another. He paused to eat and drink, tasting nothing, knowing only that the food gave him strength to continue.

He left the coliseum only once, to visit the Temple of Neptune. Magnus felt an uneasy dread in the midst of his uncertainty, as if the Fates or some jealous deity had taken a disliking to him. Neptune had been Magnus's patron god since his days as a galley slave; he made a sacrifice of seven golden coins and a lock of his hair to the deity, and breathed a humble prayer for his protection.

The morning before the feast day when he would fight Urius, Magnus slept late. His body had been honed to perfection. Rest was now more important than practice and exertion.

When he entered the gladiators' quarters to be outfitted for the day's training, the other athletes were already in the arena. The chamber was empty, save for a few attendants.

Magnus walked to the trough at the end of the room and splashed his face with cold water. He dried himself and called one of the attendants to fasten the straps of his breastplate. That done, he sat on a wooden bench and bent to tighten the buckles of his sandals.

It was then that Urius entered the chamber. His long golden hair was matted with sweat, his legs dusted with dirt from the arena.

The tall gladiator saw Magnus and smiled faintly. He approached the bench where Magnus sat, unaware of his presence. Still smiling, Urius began to strip off his gear.

His bronze breastplate struck the ground with a hollow, changing noise. Magnus started and looked up. Instantly, his breath quickened and his eyes flashed with hatred. Urius looked down at him and grinned.

"We have not seen each other for some time, Magnus. Have you been training hard for tomorrow's match?"

Magnus did not answer. He sat stiffly, grinding his teeth. He stared at Urius coldly. The gladiator was dripping with sweat. Though he smiled, he was breathing hard, as if he were winded from his early-morning practice. His eyes were slightly reddened, the pockets beneath them shadowed.

At last Magnus spoke. "Yes. And you? They say you've been training at Marcellus's estate. But it looks to me as if you've been drinking too much wine, Urius."

Urius laughed. He finished stripping the leather and bronze gear from his body and stood naked.

If Urius' face showed signs of dissipation, his body did not. His frame was as solid as ever. There was not a trace of fat around his waist, where the bands of muscles curved tight and flat. His skin, pale when Magnus had last seen him, was now golden from the sun and smooth as satin.

A curtain of sweat shimmered across his broad, hairless chest; a river of sweat poured down the sleek cleft between his pectorals and over the hard ridges of his belly. The dark blond hair between his legs was frizzled and damp; sweat dripped from the tip of his staff. The odor of his body was powerful and sharp.

Urius looked down at Magnus with a sarcastic grin. He licked his lips and nodded slowly. "You see through me, Magnus. From you I could never have any secrets. Yes, Marcellus has plied me with wine from dawn to dusk. And after dark, more wine—and boys." Urius raised one eyebrow. "I think you'll remember them. The German twins. I've been fucking them both every night."

Magnus gripped the bench tightly and forced himself not to rise, knowing that if he moved he would strike the man.

Urius seemed not to notice his tension. He was staring downward in fascination at his own crotch. His sex, always partially erect, hung outward and down from his groin, heavy and thick. Urius ran his fingertips over the blunt, bulbous head and watched the pale shaft fatten and rise in the air.

Magnus watched as well, unable to look away. Urius's shaft was prodigious. Magnus had always known that; it was one of the reasons that he hated Urius.

But now he was not feeling anger, or even envy, but something else. He was not certain what it was that he felt, but it kept him staring at the shaft that now stood hugely erect only inches from his face.

Magnus had never seen the thing so close. The long white staff was as smooth as porcelain, unmarked by veins. It was incredibly thick. Urius held it tightly in his fist, yet his fingers and thumb did not touch. Three grasping hands might barely encompass its length.

The dark blond hair nestled at its base was smooth as cornsilk, sparkling with beads of sweat. The sack that hung below was like a fist gloved in satin between Urius's thighs.

Magnus could hardly believe it possible that any man could carry something so big between his legs. And the senator Marcellus was just as large, or larger—so Erskin had said, so Magnus had seen briefly with his own eyes.

Urius kneaded the staff with his fist, drawing fresh blood into the tube, making it swell even larger. A long blue vein rose to the surface and throbbed in visible pulses.

Urius spoke in a low, sweet voice.

"Yes. I fucked them both, every day. I fucked them in the ass. I fucked them in the throat. And when they were bad . . ."

Urius gripped his shaft at the base and cupped his other hand beneath the rod. He slapped it against his palm with a loud crack.

"When they were bad, I beat them with it. They say they hate this thing in my hand. They say it hurts them. But each time they worshiped it, their own little staffs were hard as wood."

Urius sucked in a sharp breath and drew his hands away. The long stalk of flesh bobbed in the air. The long blue vein throbbed. Magnus's darting eyes followed every movement.

Urius circled his forefinger and thumb around the head of his shaft and stroked downward, midway to the base. "Erskin," he sighed, "can take it only to here, down his throat. But his brother"—he moved his hand to the very base, and then circled the balls as well—"Eskrill can swallow it all, every bit."

Urius tilted the huge shaft downward, so that it pointed directly at Magnus's face. He stepped closer, waving the staff gently from side to side. His voice was low and husky, almost a whisper.

"Put your lips where theirs have been. Kiss it. Kiss the very tip. Kiss it for me, Magnus."

Magnus held his breath. His heart seemed to have stopped beating. His head moved forward in tiny jerks as if his body tried in vain to supply the resistance that had vanished from his will.

He narrowed his eyes, but never took them from the shaft. He parted his lips and pressed his mouth against the blunt, curving tip.

The flesh was smooth as glass and warm against his lips. Above him, Urius sighed with pleasure.

"Now your tongue, Magnus. Press your tongue against the slit. I have something for you."

Magnus did as he was told, without thinking. The opening parted and the tip of his tongue slid into the hole. A discharge of semen, warm and slick, flowing over his tongue and into his mouth. The taste was musky and sweet.

Magnus moaned. He licked at the opening and mouthed the hard knob of flesh. He opened his mouth wide, until he was able to take the entire crown inside. His lips were stretched and his mouth was full. His hands moved of their own accord to his crotch and pressed against his own erection through layers of leather.

Suddenly the flesh was gone from his mouth. Urius slapped his face with it. The thing was heavy as lead.

"Tomorrow, bitch, I'll let you do more than kiss it," Urius said. His voice was as hard as steel. "Tomorrow, after I've beaten you in the arena, I'll make you crawl through the dirt on your hands and knees, like a dog, to the Emperor's box. Then you'll worship it with your mouth, for every man and woman in Rome to see. And after you've sucked it, you'll beg me to fuck you."

Magnus blinked and shook his head, dazed as if waking from a deep slumber. His cheek stung where Urius had struck him, and for a moment Magnus was paralyzed by the image Urius had planted in his mind. He saw himself on his hands and knees, whimpering, broken, begging Urius to pierce him.

Then his senses returned. His skin grew hot. His head spun with confusion and fury. He lashed out blindly and struck Urius across the thigh.

The blow would have knocked any other man to the ground. Urius only stumbled to the side, then regained his balance. He threw back his head and laughed.

Magnus looked wildly about the room. There were only two attendants in the quarters, but both were staring at him. When they saw his face, their smiles of amusement vanished.

Magnus rose and ran shaking from the room.

He walked, legs trembling, down the long, winding corridor to his apartment. He tore off his gear. His own shaft was still erect. He touched it, then drew his hand away as if stung by the pleasure of his touch.

He pulled on a coarse woolen tunic and left the coliseum, responding to the casual greetings of each gladiator he passed in the hallways with a forced stare and cold silence. He did not hear their greetings; the blood was pounding too loudly in his ears.

He walked aimlessly through the narrow, winding streets until he found himself in the great marketplace. The square was thronged with merchants and travelers who had arrived early for the great feast day and the spectacle in the coliseum.

Magnus lost himself in the crowd, hoping he would not be recognized. The humble tunic he wore might be disguise enough. Everyone knew that the greatest of gladiators could easily afford silk.

The press of the crowd only increased his agitation. It was solitude he needed. The strange welter of emotions inside him demanded silence. He tried to find his way to the Temple of Neptune, but was lost in the crowd. The cries of the hawkers and the raucous laughter of the gamblers numbed his mind. His thoughts were broken and without direction, as if he were stricken with fever.

Suddenly he collided with another body. He stepped aside and would have walked on without a word; then he saw a glint of sunlight on the shaven skull of the boy he had stumbled into. The fever flared inside him.

For an instant the boy's blue eyes met his; then Eskrill bowed his head. He blushed from the smooth dome of his head down to his neck and shoulders.

The boy was almost naked. He wore, as always, the golden bracelets around his throat and wrists. A loincloth of white silk was wrapped around his hips, pulled so low that the smoothly shaven plate of muscle below his navel was bare. Behind, the loincloth was a thin strip between his cheeks, leaving his buttocks bare.

His flesh was oiled, and more deeply tanned than when Magnus had last seen him. He was still shaven everywhere, even to his eyebrows; but Marcellus had not stopped there in tampering with his slave.

The tips of the boy's nipples were newly pierced by golden rings. A thin chain of gold was draped across his chest, suspended from ring to ring. His body was unmarked, except for an angry red welt across the side of his face, extending from his chin to his temple.

"What are you doing here?" Magnus whispered.

The boy answered, keeping his face bowed. "Marcellus brought me with him. He took Urius to the coliseum; then he brought me here. He is somewhere in the market. He told me to wait for him here."

At last the boy looked up. "Magnus, he told us of the offer he made you. Will you take it? Will you lose the match?"

It was now Magnus who looked away. "No," he said.

The boy's eyes filled with tears. "Then will you take me now? Help me escape. I don't know where I am in the city, and I can't go anywhere like this." He put his hands over his face so that Magnus would not see his tears.

"No!" Magnus said in a hoarse whisper. "Never speak of such a thing. Never even think of it! There is no escape for a slave in Rome. They would capture you within a day and kill you. They would kill anyone who helped you. They would probably kill your brother as well."

The boy slumped his shoulders and lowered his head. "Then there is no hope. Erskin said there might be, but he was wrong. Give me a knife, then, Magnus. Do you have a knife? Give it to me!"

The boy looked up. His jaw was square, his face resolved. Then he saw something beyond Magnus's shoulder, and the fire in his eyes turned to alarm.

Magnus did not have to turn to see who had approached. He heard Marcellus's voice, and felt the senator's hand on his shoulder.

"Magnus! I was about to bring Eskrill to the coliseum to visit you. We have business to discuss—or could you have forgotten? Perhaps you've changed your mind."

Magnus violently pushed the senator's hand from his shoulder. He did not dare to speak. He did not dare to touch the man. An insult or blow could cost him his life.

He could not even look at the senator. That would have been most dangerous of all. He thought of what had happened with Urius only moments before, and knew that he must escape from Marcellus. Magnus bolted into the crowd.

He heard the senator's booming voice behind him. "You are a fool, gladiator!" Then he was swallowed by the throng.

Every face he saw seemed to accuse him. Every eye seemed to penetrate his mind to glimpse the secret of what he had done with Urius, to know how deeply he was tempted to submit to Marcellus's will.


Magnus found solace at last, not at Neptune's altar, but in a tavern called The Drowned Man.

His master, Harmon, owned the tavern. The place was favored by sailors and merchants who came to the city from the harbor at Ostia. Magnus had spent much time there, after Harmon had elevated him from galley slave to household stud. Since he had become a gladiator, he had not returned to The Drowned Man. Entering it now, he could almost smell the sea.

The tavern was almost deserted. The day was sunny, and most of the sailors who might have been there had chosen the open air of the festive city over the stuffy dimness that reigned inside The Drowned Man.

Magnus took a table to himself in a shadowed corner, again hoping he would not be recognized. The last thing he desired was to talk with a stranger about the next day's match.

A buxom woman with painted eyes and lips brought him red wine. She was Greek, with broad hips and masses of inky black hair. Normally, Magnus might have done more than notice her. On another occasion, he might have solved his depression by pressing a coin into her hand and telling her to meet him upstairs in the windowless room. He had used that room countless times before, when Harmon's clumsy fingers and fumbling lips became too absurd for him to bear. But now she was an insubstantial to him as a ghost.

He had just finished his second cup of wine when a tall, bearded man rose from a table across the room and approached him.

The man wore a well-cut tunic of linen, white with an embroidered border of blue and green. He was not a common sailor. He looked familiar.

His voice was familiar as well. "Are you sure you should be drinking, Magnus? I hear that you're to fight tomorrow."

"Talloc!" Magnus said, recognizing the man at last. "Why didn't you join me when I first came in? I didn't know you, not with the fine clothes and beard."

"I recognized you, Magnus. But from the look on your face, I thought you might wish to be alone."

Magnus frowned. Then he smiled faintly. He was beginning to feel the wine.

"I did. But not with such fine company at hand. Join me. And tell me where you've been these past years. It's obvious you've come up in the world."

Talloc had been a fellow galley slave on Harmon's ship. He was a few years younger than Magnus. When Magnus had rowed beside him, they had been mere boys; Talloc had not even had a beard.

Since then Talloc had been sold twice, and had finally managed to buy his freedom. Now Talloc was a shipowner himself. He was quite willing to talk about where he had gotten the funds to begin his business.

"A wealthy Greek widow in Alexandria," he explained. "She says that my eyes make her melt." Talloc laughed. "And I don't have to ask what's become of you. Everyone from Colchis to the Pillars of Hercules has heard of Magnus the gladiator. So, screwing Harmon's ass paid off for you—and screwing Hypatia has paid off for me. The way of the world, Magnus!"

"Yes. Still, I think I envy you, Talloc."

"You, to whom every door in Rome is always open—including the door to every bedroom?"

"You're a free man, Talloc."

"But Harmon must reward you well for what you do. Don't gladiators who've done as well as you usually end up buying their freedom?"

"I've saved very little," Magnus sighed. "I've squandered most of it. Luxuries, clothes, a chariot. Boys. Living like a wealthy man when I'm no more than a slave. Perhaps in a year or two I could save enough gold to buy myself from Harmon. If I haven't been killed in the arena first."

"Is that what worries you—tomorrow's match? You know, I've never seen you fight, only heard of you—though I'll be seeing you tomorrow, since we don't sail for Byzantium until the morning after. But they say that Magnus in the arena is like a lion, a man without fear."

"Perhaps they lie," Magnus said. "But it is more than that, Talloc. More than gold and death and slavery that oppresses me now."

"You are weary of your life." Talloc's face was somber.

"I think I am."

"Well, for the gods' sake, don't become a Christian. That's what seems to happen to people these days, when they become as glum as you are. Then they stay glum, and talk about nothing but death and suffering. They're bad medicine, bad for the Empire. Believe me, I know. My wife has been harboring a whole coven of them in Alexandria. They smell like pigs and eat like them too, and they're totally worthless. Hypatia wants to give them our money. They say she'll be punished after she dies if she doesn't hand over the gold. Imagine such a thing! It's witchcraft. Oriental witchcraft."

Magnus grimaced at the idea of himself joining a cult. "Don't worry, Talloc. Neptune has always protected me, and I am loyal to him."

Talloc sipped his wine and became pensive. "Perhaps it was Neptune who watched over you when we were slaves together, Magnus, but it was you who protected me. I haven't forgotten what you did for me in the old days. You saved my life, not once but three times. The pirates off Chios—yes, you remember, you're smiling now. What a fight that was! And the time the ship caught fire a few miles out of Antioch, and you ripped my chains from the deck. I could have been burned alive."

Talloc lowered his voice. "And the time the galley master beat me because I wouldn't sleep with him. You tried to stop him and took twenty lashes yourself. I think the pain would have killed me if it had gone on much longer. That, especially, I haven't forgotten."

Magnus's smile vanished. The memory of that cruel punishment made him think of the German twins, and their lives with Marcellus. He remembered how the galley master had used him—and he thought of Urius's rod in his mouth . . .

"Magnus," Talloc said gravely, "if there is ever anything I can do to repay you—any favor, great or small, ask it of me. If there is anything I can do now—ask me."

Magnus shook his head. "No, you can't help. But someday, perhaps, I'll need a friend, and I'll remember you. Talloc, you are a good man." Magnus smiled ruefully. "An opportunist, perhaps, but who is not? I've met few good men lately. I have moved among evil men. I'm glad I came here and saw you again. I'm glad that you've prospered."

The serving woman came to refill his cup, but Magnus covered it with his hand. "I have to go now, Talloc. You're right, I don't need the wine. And I want to visit the Temple of Neptune. Besides," he grinned, "the way the serving woman has been watching you, I don't think you'll lack for company after I'm gone.

The weather for the feast day was perfect. The sky was cloudless. The sun was bright but mild.

Magnus stayed alone in his apartment long after the games and races began. He did not wish to see Urius more than he had to, or to be bothered by Marcellus. A night without sex or dreams had readied him for the fight.

He waited until an hour before the match before he left his room and walked to the athletes' quarters.

A few of the other gladiators smiled at him oddly. The attendants had spread gossip of his weakness on the previous day, or more likely, ·

Urius himself had boasted of it and pointed to the slaves as witness, but no one was brash enough to taunt him.

Magnus limbered his muscles, honed his blade, and summoned an attendant to massage him and help him dress. Only minutes before the match, a well-groomed, middle-aged eunuch approached him and thrust a rolled parchment before his face.

"What is that?" Magnus growled, tempted to strike the servant for his insolence. Then he saw that the man wore a collar of gold, and knew that he had come from Marcellus.

"Can you read?" the eunuch asked in a reedy voice.

"No."

"Then I am instructed to read this aloud to you." The eunuch unrolled the parchment and cleared his throat. "The message reads: 'My offer stands. Do you accept? Make your mark upon the parchment.'"

The eunuch offered him a wax pencil.

Magnus took the parchment and glanced at the odd markings. He did not take the pencil. Instead, he crumpled the paper into a ball and spat on it.

"Take this back to your master," he said.

Magnus returned his attention to his whetstone and sword.

He did not see the eunuch turn toward Urius and raise one finger.

He did not see the smile on Urius's face, or the vial of thick blue liquid that Urius took from a pouch beside his feet.

Urius uncorked the vial. Careful not to breath its fumes or to let the liquid touch his flesh, he poured the viscous contents onto a cloth, then smeared it over the points of his trident.

The liquid dried quickly and became invisible.

# – Eight –

The match began well. Urius's long debauch in the countryside had slowed his reflexes, and Magnus quickly scored a number of superficial wounds to the gladiator's legs and arms. Such early blows were usually prophetic of victory to come.

Urius finally managed to strike him. Even so, it was only a glancing and insubstantial blow. Urius did not lunge with the trident, but swung it like a scythe. The glistening razorlike points grazed Magnus's belly. Three thin marks were left across the skin, barely deep enough to draw blood.

The wounds stung, but were easily forgotten in the excitement of the fight. After a moment they ceased to sting altogether, and instead became strangely numb.

Later, Magnus realized that his entire belly had grown cold.

The coldness spread to his chest and groin. As the sensation reached his limbs, a wave of nausea coursed through him and his stomach began to cramp.

He continued to fight. Soon it was impossible for him to land a blow against Urius. It was the best he could do to fend off the jabbing trident and the net that seemed to constantly hover over his head, waiting to snare him.

Soon he could not do even that. Urius began to strike blows against him. The blows were glancing, the wounds small, but wherever the trident cut him, the feeling disappeared from his flesh.

Magnus began to feel what he had not felt in the arena since his earliest days as a gladiator: panic. A surge of fear, colder than the numbness in his chest and limbs, eddied through him.

Urius was jeering at him from behind the helmet he wore. Magnus could hear the words, but could not understand them. The numbness had spread to his brain.

*Slaves of the Empire*
Published by The Haworth Press, Inc., 2006. All rights reserved.
doi:10.1300/5502_08

Then there was a loud clanging noise, like brazen gates crashing shut, and Magnus's sword was wrenched from his grasp.

Something struck his chest, and then the net was everywhere around him. The chafing cords pulled painfully tight against his face and throat. His arms were locked to his sides. His ankles were drawn together and he fell upon his hip.

A kick at his groin rolled him onto his back. Urius's foot was upon his chest, crushing him. The blond gladiator was a giant above him. Urius lifted his trident and aimed it at Magnus's throat.

The roar of the crowd was deafening, hysterical, hostile. Magnus rolled his eyes upward and strained to see the Imperial box.

He saw Marcellus there, sitting at the Emperor's left, whispering into the old man's ear. The Emperor nodded and raised his fist.

Magnus could not make out the signal. The crowd was angry, hissing. Magnus writhed in panic and felt his bowels grow loose. He looked up and saw the trident descending.

It landed in the sand before his face. The judgment had been thumbs-up.

Two Nubians, wearing golden collars around their throats, came to drag him from the arena. The crowd continued to scream and jeer; many a betting man's fortune had been lost that day.

The Nubians dragged him close by the wall. Men and women leaned over the railing to spit down at him and curse.

They pulled him into the passageway that led to the athletes' quarters. The gladiators were huddled together. Their faces were blank with shock. Those who had been closest to Magnus turned their heads away in shame. How could he have fought so poorly?

Harmon was there. He was behaving like a madman, screaming and tearing his hair. He kicked Magnus in the belly as the Nubians dragged him by.

They pulled him past the gladiators' quarters and outside the coliseum. They lifted him like a heavy sack and dropped him into a waiting litter. The curtains were dropped, sealing him from view.

The litter jerked and began to move. Magnus lost consciousness.

He dreamed. His dreams were nightmares. He dreamed that Urius had made good his threat to publicly debase him after the fight.

Magnus saw himself naked in the arena, crawling on his hands and knees after Urius and his giant shaft. Urius taunted him with it, offering it to him to suck, then drawing it away before he could touch it with his lips, making him groan with frustration. The crowd was not jeering, but laughing.

He looked up and saw Neptune, huge in the sky above, waving a vast trident covered with blue seaweed. Magnus lifted his arms and cried out to the god—then saw that it was not Neptune looming above him, but Marcellus, dressed in his general's garb, the spangle of coins across his chest bright like miniature suns. Marcellus looked down with his grim smile and raised the hem of his garment. He took his shaft in his hand and began to urinate, and his urine was a great jet of seawater, crashing onto Magnus with the force of stone, flooding and filling the arena to the shrieks of the mob. Magnus was adrift in the salty flow, thrown back and forth by churning waves, then sucked into the frenzied spiral of a vast, dark whirlpool.

Suddenly he was a boy again, a galley slave, naked on his hands and knees in the galley master's cabin like so many times before. The galley master sat in his great oaken chair, legs apart, eyes red with wine, his big shaft standing straight between his thighs. "Crawl to me, boy. You do it so much better than all the rest, even if I do have to beat you. Crawl to me and take it in your mouth."

Magnus crept toward the big man, hungry and hating himself for his hunger—but it was no longer the galley master who sat enthroned before him. It might have been Marcellus. It might have been Urius. It made no difference. They were the same man.

The litter lurched and came to a halt. Magnus woke. Still, he could hardly tell his dreams from the strange unreality of the cool twilight.

The Nubians lifted him from the litter. Urius's net was left tight around him, but his legs were cut free. The black slaves held his arms and pulled him, stumbling, into the portico of a great marble house.

The busts that lined the hallway were familiar. Grim, unsmiling faces—he was in Marcellus's house.

Why?

He was led into the atrium. The illumination from the skylight above was fading, but there was enough light for him to take in the scene in an instant.

Urius was there. He stood naked, wet from the bath. Below him, Erskin was on his knees, crouching low between the gladiator's thighs. His hands were twisted behind his back and tied to his ankles. His mouth was stuffed with Urius's balls.

The gladiator's head was thrown back, his lips parted. He held his shaft in both hands, squeezing and stroking it.

Urius lowered his face as Magnus was brought in. He bared his teeth and hissed with pleasure.

Erskin turned his head as much as he could. He saw Magnus and blushed. His cheeks bulged, his chin was glossy with spit. His penis was stiff, pointing upward from his groin like a handle. He shut his eyes tightly.

Nearby, Marcellus lay naked on a low divan. He wore the pectoral of golden coins across his chest. Cushions were propped beneath his head and shoulders. In one hand he held a short, stiff leather crop.

Eskrill was standing over him, facing him. His legs were spread wide to straddle the divan. His hands were lashed together and bound to the chain that connected his nipples, so that he stood in the attitude of a supplicant in prayer. His ass was impaled on Marcellus's shaft.

He bobbed obscenely up and down, riding the thick mallet of flesh. He rose up until the mouth of his ass gripped the crown, then plunged downward until his cheeks rested on his master's thighs and the huge shaft was swallowed by his bowels.

The boy was covered with sweat. Every muscle in his lean, hairless body was tense. The veins in his neck and forehead stood out like cords from the strain of the ordeal. His face was bright red. His mouth was open wide, drooling saliva. His eyes were shut.

He shook his head from side to side, grunting and moaning. His short, slender shaft was hard as stone. It slapped with a sweaty crack against his belly and thighs as he rode Marcellus's iron.

Beneath him, his master was splayed on the divan like a big cat lazing in the sun. Marcellus's eyes were half-open, dreamy with pleasure.

His lips were pursed. Occasionally he lifted the crop and struck the boy's thigh to speed the fucking.

Marcellus reached for Eskrill's balls and squeezed them tightly. He pulled the boy's staff downward and stopped its jerking. He looked at the rod of flesh for a moment, then raised the crop and struck the head of Eskrill's penis.

The boy sobbed loudly. He shuddered and paused for an instant, then fucked himself more frantically on his master's shaft.

Marcellus stretched and grunted with pleasure. He struck the boy's penis again, then his balls, then his chest and face.

The senator turned his head and looked at Magnus. His eyes raked over the gladiator's body. This was Marcellus at his pleasure, drunk with ecstasy and power. The look in his eyes made Magnus cringe.

Marcellus threw the crop aside. He lifted Eskrill by his hips and pulled the boy off his shaft with a loud popping noise, then pushed him away. Eskrill's hands flew from his chest, seeking balance and pulling on the rings that pierced each nipple. He fell trembling to the hard marble floor.

Marcellus stood. His lips were parted, drawn back to show his teeth, but he did not smile. He walked to Magnus, placed his hands upon his shoulders, and pushed him roughly to the floor. He lifted his foot to Magnus's face and forced him backward until he was prostrate on the marble.

Above him, Magnus could not see the senator's face, only his sturdy legs and his upright shaft, hard as wood and moist from the heat of Eskrill's ass. Then Urius took his place beside Marcellus, a second pair of legs, a second shaft looming above him, dark and enormous in the gray light, like an object seen through murky water, blurred and magnified. A thread of semen oozed from the tip of Urius's shaft and fell with a soft slap against Magnus's eyes, clotting his lashes, blinding him.

He could not see. He could barely hear; there was a sudden ringing in his ears, like the clangor of a thousand swords against a thousand shields. Then through the din he heard Urius speak.

"Open your mouth!"

He did nothing, paralyzed and senseless on the cold floor. Then something struck him between the legs, and he opened his mouth in silent pain. A dollop of warm semen fell upon his tongue, slick and musky, and for the second time he tasted Urius in his mouth.

Above him two voices spoke, but they seemed to be the same voice, the monologue of a monster speaking to itself.

"He is ours now."

"At last . . ."

"But how quickly will he break?"

"He will be broken before morning. . . ."

There was a blow to his side, a kick that sent him rolling and then falling with a splash into the warm waters of the pool. He heard the waters close over him with a liquid slap, felt himself strike bottom with a gentle thud, felt his body dissolve into the warm murkiness, and thought he heard the muffled din of swords striking shields.

# – Nine –

For long hours Magnus slept but did not sleep. He became one with the swirling warm waters of the pool, dissolved into darkness, became a thing without shape or mass. Yet he vaguely felt the touch of hands upon his body, the stretching and turning of limbs he could not command to move.

The surface of his body was alive with strange muted sensations—a rough scraping across his flesh with the friction of porous stones, then a tightness around him like taut bandages, pulled away from his body with a biting adhesive tug. The scraping and the stinging were everywhere, on his face, across his chest, under his arms and between his legs. He felt no pain, only the constant manipulation of his body as he was turned, stretched, twisted, scraped, and pulled at.

Even these sensations ceased after a time, and he felt nothing but an unaccustomed coolness across his chest and between his legs. Then he was being pulled up by his arms until he was upright, half standing on extended toes, suspended by his arms.

Little by little he awoke.

His head was held upright by something cold and metallic around his neck. At first he could only struggle to open his eyes, blinking wearily as if a soft weight rested on the lids. Candlelight surrounded him; the gentle illumination seeped into his eyes, nudging him into consciousness.

Before him stood Urius, naked. His blond mane was golden in the warm candle glow. The planes of his face were perfect and smooth like polished marble after the sculptor's touch. His eyes shone. His broad mouth was curved into a sensuous smile, inviting and almost friendly.

"So, the newest pleasure slave of the great Senator Marcellus is finally awake." Urius smiled more broadly and stepped toward him. He raised his hand and Magnus flinched—but the touch was gentle, be-

*Slaves of the Empire*
Published by The Haworth Press, Inc., 2006. All rights reserved.
doi:10.1300/5502_09

ginning at the hollow of his throat and running with oily smoothness down his chest and belly. Magnus strained to move, and could not; his body was bound in the shape of an X, arms and legs extended and held fast in the posture of slaves crucified upon the cross. At Urius's touch, a shudder of apprehension and strange excitement ran through him.

Urius was gazing at his chest. "Oh, Magnus, I have always wanted to see you like this. So naked and smooth. So ready to be broken upon your master's rod."

He brought his face close. The smell of wine was sweet upon his breath; the fumes rose into Magnus's nostrils and seemed to blur his senses. Then Urius's mouth was upon his lips in a savage kiss. Magnus held his mouth tightly shut, until Urius's fingernails closed upon his nipples, biting fiercely into the flesh. He opened his mouth to gasp, and found himself succumbing to the kiss, allowing Urius to enter him with his tongue.

Urius's groin was against him. The pressure of his body was strong and warm, setting off a flood of heat through the strangely sensitive flesh between Magnus's legs. He felt his own shaft begin to harden.

Magnus wrenched his head back, pulling free of the kiss, confused and frightened.

Urius still smiled, undisturbed. He tugged at Magnus' nipples; then his touch softened once more like a caress. "You look so frightened, Magnus, like a little boy about to weep. But you needn't fear me now—we're no longer enemies, you and I. All that is past. I have won and you have lost. You have lost everything." Urius raised an eyebrow at some secret thought. "Perhaps not quite everything. But the time for that will come."

Urius turned to fetch something from a low table beside him. Magnus looked about the room. He was no longer in the atrium, nor in the stables, but in some other, unfamiliar chamber. There was a low canopied bed to his right, hung with sheer silks and strewn with cushions. Before him was a long wall covered by a black curtain, and to his left a standing polycandelion ablaze with light. Above him he could see only his own arms, the wrists encased in golden bracelets linked to chains extending upward into darkness.

Urius turned back to him. Between his hands he clenched a long, slender golden wire. He reached down, toward Magnus's sex; Magnus strained to see but he could not. He knew it must be a shining collar of gold that held his jaw upright.

Urius was handling his shaft and balls, tying them at the base with the wire, so tight it seemed to cut through him. He spoke in a low, coddling, voice, as a man might speak to a child who must endure a harsh but inevitable ordeal.

"Once we were rivals, Magnus, and I hated you just as you hated me. But the game is over. There is no longer any need for animosity, for jealousy. We can be friends now, Magnus. And believe me, in this house you will need a friend."

Urius finished his handiwork. There was a slight tightness between Magnus's legs; his genitals were bloated and pinched. He pulled against his bonds in a rush of frustration. He fought to keep his voice from breaking.

"But how?" he whispered. "Why—"

Urius struck him across the face with a blow that brought blood to his lips. "You will speak when you're told to speak, or else I'll have your tongue torn out. The better to fuck your throat."

Urius strode to the curtained wall and pulled the drapery aside. "Look at yourself, gladiator!"

Behind the curtain was a huge mirror of burnished silver. Magnus gazed upon his wavering reflection in the reddish glow from the polycandelion and groaned.

He stood spread-eagled, his feet pulled far apart and cuffed to bolts in the floor, his arms pulled apart and so high that he was forced onto his toes. Wrapped around his neck, his wrists, and ankles were bracelets of gold. Apart from these, and the gold wire tied cutting-tight around the base of his sex, he was naked—and more than that . . .

He was a stranger to the body bound and collared before him in the mirror. The sight of it shocked him and filled him with a terrible excitement. They had denuded him, removed every hair from his body.

His awesome musculature had been rendered impotent. The broad shoulders and slab-muscled chest, the tight waist and massive thighs were his. But the flesh was now a woman's flesh, or a boy's, smooth and full, naked and inviting, covered with a mist of oil. The heavy flesh of his pectorals glistened obscenely in the candlelight, the nipples shining like points of liquid copper. Even his face was not his own. They had removed his beard, oiled his cheeks, and reddened his lips with henna.

But worst was what they had done to his sex. They had shaved it, bound it with wire, exaggerated and made a mockery of it, turned it from a proud weapon into a toy. It no longer seemed to grow from his body, but seemed instead attached to it, vulnerable and exposed, a bloated tube tied at the base and suspended from the smooth delta of flesh below his navel.

The sight of it shamed him; yet it made his breath grow quick with excitement. He remembered his first sight of Eskrill's denuded shaft at the coliseum, when Marcellus had exposed the boy in public, and the way Eskrill had blushed and turned his face away.

Urius stood beside him. He ran one hand over the sleek plates of Magnus's chest and the other over his shoulders and back, down to the cleavage of his ass. A finger probed between his buttocks and touched the opening there; and from the strangeness of the touch, Magnus knew they had denuded him there as well. The finger, oiled from its glide down his spine, toyed at his entrance and then slipped inside.

Magnus worked his lips soundlessly and shivered. A wave of submission eddied through his bowels like warm wine. Magnus had known the sensation before—known it, hated it, craved it. He had prayed to never know it again. The finger moving inside him took him back in time, stripped away the shield that years of blood and fame had built around him He was a slave, after all, and to be a slave was to be an object, fit for fondling or the touch of a master's whip, for being decorated with gold bracelets and stripped of everything that might disguise him as a man. Magnus gazed at the stranger in the mirror and watched his denuded shaft grow thicker and longer until it stood upright, submissive and vulnerable.

The finger moved inside him, loosened him, made him ready for more—and then withdrew. Urius stepped behind him. Magnus clenched

his fists and prepared for the penetration, remembering, praying that he
would not be broken by the pain.

He felt it, blunt and warm, nudging between his buttocks and then
pushing against his fundament. Urius's hands were upon him, pinching his nipples, gliding over his belly, finally gripping the cradle of his
hipbones with bruising force. Urius's breath was in his ear, hot and
fragrant with wine.

"How long has it been, Magnus, since you were taken by another
man? How long since a shaft made its way inside you and opened you
up, made you squeal and writhe like a woman and beg to be fucked?"

Magnus did not answer. The bluntness moved against him, forcing
the hole inward upon itself. Magnus stiffened with dread. It was too
big, too big . . .

"How long, Magnus? Answer me! Who was the last man to take
you?"

The pressure increased. Magnus gasped. "The galley master," he
whispered. "The galley master . . ."

"Yes, the wizened old bag of a galley master, when you were a slave
on Harmon's ship. He fucked you often, didn't he? Fucked the pretty
young slaveboy in the mouth. In the ass. Easy to see why. You have a
beautiful body, Magnus. A beautiful face. A shame to have covered it
so long with a beard. When I first saw you, that first day in the gladiators' quarters, I knew I would have you. You were different from the
others, so proud, so quiet, like a little boy in a strong man's body. I
knew you despised me. Knew I would have to wait . . ."

The head of Urius's shaft was suddenly inside him, impaling him
like the point of a spear. Magnus shuddered and strained against his
bonds.

"Some men were born to dominate, Magnus. Some were meant to
offer up their bodies in submission. Between your days as Harmon's
galley slave and this night, all has been a lie. The dream of glory and
freedom was only a dream. This is your life and your purpose. To be a
pleasure slave. To offer up your mouth and your ass—to me."

Magnus groaned and gritted his teeth, fighting back tears. Whatever had happened, however it had happened, it was done. His bondage proved it. What Urius said was true.

Urius reached around him and clutched his shaft, erect in bondage. "You want me to take you, don't you, Magnus?"

Magnus gazed at his reflection, shut his eyes and did not answer.

"You do. And I want to take you, Magnus. I will. But not yet. Marcellus will want you first. Then he will let me have you. I like it that way. Do you know why? When Marcellus is done using his horsecock on you, you'll be swollen and bruised inside; the mouth of your ass will be aching and raw. That's the way I like it best—to fuck a hole that's already sore and stinging, to feel the swollen veins inside you throbbing against my shaft. To feel you cringe with each stroke. An ordeal greater even than with Marcellus. You'll squeal like a pig and whimper and beg me to stop, and you'll call me master."

"No!"

"Yes!" Urius hissed in his ear, and suddenly drove the shaft all the way into him. Magnus shrieked and jerked wildly against his bonds.

It was over in an instant. Urius withdrew his shaft until only the head was inside him. But the pain was like a whiplash, still stinging his bowels, deeper than the galley master had ever reached.

Urius seized a handful of Magnus's hair and jerked his head back. His voice was wild and breathless. "You must never contradict me, Magnus. You will anger me, and you will suffer for it. See what you've made me do? You've made me spear you with it. But it was only a taste; you'll still be tight for Marcellus. Now let me prepare you for him and be done with it."

Urius was still, then, and ominously quiet. Then he sighed—and Magnus's mind, fogged with pain, suddenly flashed with apprehension. He knew why Urius's shaft was still inside him.

It began with a quick, bolting rush of warmth, just inside the mouth of his fundament. The rush mounted upward inside him, swirling and searing hot against the bruises Urius had left deep within. Then the pressure began, and the intimation of a cramp in his groin. Behind him, Urius sighed with satisfaction as he flooded Magnus's bowels.

Higher and higher the flow churned, bloating him and ballooning his bowels with its force. He fought to eject it, but it stayed inside him, plugged by the head of Urius's shaft. Urius was laughing behind him. "Tighten the mouth of your ass, now," he hissed. "Close it tight, as if you were kissing my shaft farewell." He slapped both hands against Magnus's cheeks, making the ring of muscle clamp shut.

The head of Urius's shaft popped free, and just as quickly he was pushing something else inside, another plug to hold the liquid. It was tapered and smooth, small at first and then flaring larger, then abruptly small again, so that the lips closed over it and held it fast.

Urius walked in front of him, still laughing, his shaft standing proudly erect. He struck Magnus in the stomach with his fist. Magnus clawed the air as the cramp exploded in his belly. He felt his body contort, struggling to bend double from the pain but held upright by the chains. His mind was blurred by the heaving pressure inside him, the urgent need to empty himself. His flesh erupted in cold sweat.

"Now, Magnus, you must be properly outfitted to meet your new master." Urius turned to the low table and picked up two odd pieces of jewelry, like a courtesan's earrings, two teardrops of ebony attached to golden screws. Urius attached them to the very tips of Magnus's nipples, tightening the sharp screws until the flesh was pinched into points. The ebony pendants dangled heavily from the high ridge of his pectorals, pulling his nipples into tiny cones of pain.

Urius fetched a third jewel, another ebony teardrop, but much larger and threaded at the top with a thin golden wire like the one that separated Magnus's sex from his body. He tied it to Magnus's shaft, just behind the meaty ridge that defined the head. The thin wire cut into him, disappearing into the flesh. The heavy pendant dragged the shaft downward, bending his erection into a snout that pointed toward the floor.

Urius stood beside him and wrenched his head back by a fist in his hair, forcing him to open eyes blurred with pain.

"Look in the mirror, slave. What do you see?"

Magnus gazed at his reflection, and in that moment something broke inside him. He saw a pleasure slave wracked with pain but erect nonetheless, nude and hairless, legs open and trembling, nipples and penis hung with jewels, mouth crudely rouged, like a whore's mouth. And beside him stood the man who had done these things to him: the great gladiator Urius, tall, muscular, and blond, smiling and stroking his great shaft in one hand, the shaft that had bruised him with a single stroke and then filled his bowels with piss.

In his other hand Urius now held a long, thin switch, a sapling branch stripped of its bark. There was a sound of ruptured air, and then it landed with a crack across Magnus's belly, then his chest, his back, his thighs, and ass, striping his nakedness with long, thin welts. Urius deftly wielded it against the tip of each nipple, held erect by the pointed golden screws. He whipped it against the swollen plum-red head of Magnus's shaft, stinging the parted lips like a bee, making him shriek with pain.

Magnus screamed. He whimpered. His body spasmed and jerked against his will, like a puppet performing a grotesque dance of pain at his master's bidding. Finally he wept, and the tears were like acid on his cheeks, scarring him with shame.

Soon Magnus's body was thatched with lash marks from his ankles to his wrists, his flesh an envelope of pain. Then Urius concentrated on his sex, grasping it tightly at the base, pulling upward till Magnus was suspended from Urius's fist, his feet pulled clear of the floor. Urius rotated his wrist, twisting the shaft upside-down and exposing Magnus's testicles to the switch. He whipped the reddened knob of flesh with a cruel relentless rhythm in time with Magnus's screams; and in time the screams turned to words, as Magnus begged him to stop. But Urius was not satisfied until Magnus called him master, and even then he prolonged the torment, lashing the twisted testicles and the tender underside of Magnus's sex, watching his exhausted body dance with pain.

Urius was merciful at last. The whipping stopped. Then, to the sound of a turning winch, Magnus was lowered to a crouch and pulled backward by his hips. Urius removed the plug and held a bronze ewer below to catch the eruption. As the urine gushed out of him and the cramps subsided, Magnus felt himself emptied of all will, all resistance. He gave only the slightest moan as another plug was pushed into him, a small leather ball hung with strips of leather like a horse tail.

Urius lowered him further, onto his knees. The formula was unspoken but inevitable: The pleasure slave would now grovel before his master's rod. Urius's shaft was before him, huge and perfectly formed, smooth and unblemished, like a thick mallet carved from ivory. It was white with blushes of pink, the color of cream and roses. Magnus gazed up at the perfect beam of flesh, and beyond, at Urius's belly, flat and hard as a shield, and his pectorals, rising from his chest like plates of crystal. Above, the face of his tormentor hovered in the candlelight, as beautiful and distant and alien as the face of a god.

Urius held his shaft proudly in his fist, like a cudgel, and rubbed it over Magnus's upturned face, smearing the tears that streamed over hollowed cheeks. He pulled his shaft back, pushed Magnus's face to one side and slapped him with it. He commanded Magnus to kiss it, and Magnus closed his eyes and pressed his lips to the beveled crown. He ordered Magnus to lick it, and Magnus obeyed, running his tongue over the warm, silky flesh. He commanded Magnus to open his mouth; and after tracing the circled lips with the tip of his shaft, he entered him.

He fucked Magnus's face with a gentle, easy rhythm at first, stretching his lips wide with the bulk of his sex and stroking it in and out of his mouth. Then Urius sighed with pleasure above him, and a small foretaste of semen oozed onto Magnus's tongue; and the breakage inside Magnus was shattered into fragments.

He lurched forward and impaled his throat on Urius's sex, suddenly desperate to give it pleasure. He sucked it frantically, choking himself on it, drawing back to gaze upon it and rub his face against it, then catching it with his lips and swallowing it whole, opening himself so that Urius could brutally rape his throat at will.

The primal logic of master and slave overcame him, making him an accomplice in his own degradation. It was right that Urius should be standing over him, strangling him with his cock. It was right that Magnus should grovel naked at his feet with a tail dangling from his ass. His throat was a sheath; Urius was the sword. All must be in balance. Urius's pleasure must equal his pain. Urius's triumph must equal his own humiliation.

Urius groaned loudly above him, and Magnus groaned in response, hungry to feel the mallet pulse in his throat and empty itself into his belly. He would gag on it, and Urius would know ecstasy—but Urius pulled back, wrenching the shaft from his mouth, robbing him of the moment. The shaft jerked before him and sprayed his face with long, glistening ropes of semen.

Magnus opened his mouth wide; Urius slapped his face. "Greedy bitch," he growled, spraying more semen on his face and slapping him again—and Magnus remembered Zenobius on his hands and knees in the gladiators' quarters. He did not draw his face away but offered it up for Urius to batter first with his hand, then with his cock, slapping heavy and wet across his open mouth until his lips were bruised.

Urius stepped back. He circled the slave at his feet. While Magnus still groaned in frustration, Urius, breathing heavily and smiling in triumph, released his wrists from the chains.

In that moment Magnus might have fought back. His feet were still bound, but he could at least have resisted when Urius wrenched his hand behind his back and chained the two golden bracelets together. Once his arms were bound, Urius released his ankles. Magnus might have run. Instead he did not, staying locked in the posture of a slave on his knees.

Urius circled him slowly, still catching his breath. He flicked the switch against the welts he had made earlier, nodding his approval as Magnus flinched and hissed with pain.

"Now you are ready, I think. Through the door." Urius pointed with the switch.

Magnus began to crawl awkwardly on his knees. A blow from the switch across his face stopped him. "Not like that," Urius said. "You will go to him on your feet. Stand up!"

# – Ten –

Magnus straightened his body. His legs were weak; his head spun with dizziness. He began to walk, and again Urius struck him.

"Not like that," he said. "I see we will have to teach you everything. Spread your legs apart and bend your knees. Now up on your toes. Chest out, ass up so that he can see the tail. See in the mirror, how the posture flatters you? This is how Marcellus likes to be approached by his slaves. Now walk!" The switch lashed out and raised a fresh welt across his buttocks.

Thus Magnus was paraded through the dark, empty hallways, Urius behind him, stinging him with the switch when his posture grew weak, forcing him to stay on his toes and take short, mincing steps, ordering him to swing his tail and the weight suspended from his shaft from side to side. His nipples and his sex and the ball inside him felt huge, out of all proportion.

They passed through the long hallway lined by the busts of Marcellus's ancestors. The stony faces seemed to watch his slow, tortuous progress with grim amusement; Magnus could almost hear their scornful laughter, and was grateful when they stepped out of the house, into the portico that led to the stables, where the only noise was the soughing of crickets beneath the blanket of night and the rasping of his own labored breathing—and the whoosh of air followed by a sharp crack each time Urius struck him with the switch.

They entered the stable and descended the long flight of stairs; and Magnus knew that he had taken only the first step in a long journey toward annihilation.

Marcellus sat upon a gilded chair on a raised marble platform beside the great brazier in the center of the room. He wore only a sleeve-

*Slaves of the Empire*
Published by The Haworth Press, Inc., 2006. All rights reserved.
doi:10.1300/5502_10

less Egyptian robe of transparent black silk. Its delicacy was incongruous against the rugged mass of his trunk and limbs. The robe was belted at the waist and parted over his thighs; his shaft hung meaty and thick over the edge of the chair.

His face was half in shadow—his brooding eyes hidden in darkness, his grim jaw and frowning lips revealed by the light of the brazier.

Magnus stood before him. His legs trembled with exhaustion, but each time he dropped onto his heels Urius struck him with the switch, forcing him back on his toes. His body was covered with sweat. His eyes were misted, looking inward upon his pain.

"He is broken?" Marcellus said. His voice was cold and even.

"Yes."

"So quickly . . ."

"I knew it would be easy. From the moment he first tasted my shaft, the day before the match . . ."

Marcellus was content to simply sit and gaze upon him for a long moment. The senator's shaft grew longer and doubled in thickness. It rose from the seat of the chair.

"On your knees, Magnus."

Magnus knelt, almost falling; his legs had lost their marrow.

"Crawl to me, slave, and take my balls in your mouth."

Marcellus lifted his shaft aside, exposing his testicles, huge and loose in their sack. Magnus crept forward and touched his lips against the soft pouch, and Marcellus used his fingers to stuff both balls into his mouth. Magnus's cheeks were bloated like udders.

The hugeness of Marcellus's sex unmanned him, made him feel submissive and weak. The man's shaft was impossibly massive and heavy across his face, covering one eye. With the other Magnus looked upward, straining to meet Marcellus's shadowed eyes, able only to see his mouth, the lips glistening with wine in the firelight.

Marcellus began without preamble. "Your master Harmon—your former master—has suffered a very bad year, Magnus. Did you not know? Were you too busy with your boys and your fame to see his desperation? Ships looted and lost at sea; warehouses set ablaze; more cargoes destroyed than delivered. All accidents, of course. The web of the Fates. Catastrophe after catastrophe, creditors and litigants ha-

ranguing him like harpies, until you were the only thriving invest-
ment he had left. The only property with which he could gamble to
save himself . . . Use your tongue, slave."

Magnus could hardly obey, so stuffed was his mouth. Marcellus's
testicles moved inside his cheeks, enormous and alive.

"Harmon was forced to borrow heavily. From bankers at first, finally from me. Many times he has had to kiss the hem of my robe in
gratitude for my generosity. But charity has a limit. Debts must be re-
paid. I told him my price: Magnus the gladiator. He stalled for time.
When he learned of the match with Urius he saw his only hope. All he
had left he wagered on your victory today. Now Harmon is ruined . . .
and you are mine."

The shaft resting on Magnus's face grew large and heavier, then
rose into the air above his eyes, blocking all else from sight.

"Did you think I would really let you have the German twins,
Magnus? Never. You were as great a fool as I thought. They were
only the lure. You see, I wanted you to lose the match with Urius of
your own free will. I wanted you to know, each day of your life, that
you had brought yourself to this place by your own stupidity and lust.
But you kept your precious honor. It does not matter; honor will
mean nothing to you after this night."

Marcellus pushed Magnus's mouth from his balls and presented his
shaft. "Look at it, slave. Gaze upon the favor of the gods."

Magnus stared at the shaft in awe and suppressed a sob. The thing
was bigger even than Urius's—longer, immensely thicker, dark and
swollen with blood. The flesh was thin, almost translucent, knotted
with blue veins. It was not a thing of beauty, like Urius's shaft, but
obscenely ugly, its hugeness almost a deformity.

"Take the head in your mouth."

Marcellus demanded the impossible. Magnus pulled back, and felt
the switch against his shoulder, then on the palms of his hands and
the soles of his feet. He opened his mouth wide and forced his lips
against the crown.

"Wider!" Marcellus barked, reaching down to squeeze his chin and
pull him forward. Magnus's jaw reached its limit—and then his lips
slid over the head. The knob of flesh was within him.

Marcellus sat back, satisfied. "Enough. You will learn to take more of it, in time. You cannot imagine it, can you, having the whole thing stuffed down your throat. But you will learn. By slow degrees, I will teach you to swallow it. And that is how you will die, Magnus, when the time comes and I've grown weary of you. I will have your teeth pulled and your jawbone broken, and I will simply force it all the way into your throat and neck, and leave it there while you strangle to death."

Marcellus sighed and the shaft began to spill liquid into the back of Magnus's throat. Magnus trembled with relief, thinking the man had somehow reached his climax; but it was not semen pouring into his throat. Magnus swallowed to keep from choking; and all the time Marcellus spoke, the urine flowed into his mouth, not in a single rush, but from time to time starting and stopping, allowing him to swallow before feeding him more, like an obscene parody of an infant nursing on a nipple.

Marcellus's voice was low and dreamlike. "Within a week, Magnus, I shall be the Emperor of all Rome. I tell you this now, so that you will know your place from the beginning. There has never been anything I have wanted that I have not achieved. I married the daughter of the richest senator in Rome. I won glory in Spain to rival Caesar's. I have made the world's greatest gladiator my toy. And within a week I shall be master of the Empire.

"All is planned. There is not the slightest possibility of error. In seven days the Emperor will be brought to ruin—found in his bath, his wrists slit by his own hand—and the Senate of Rome will declare me First Citizen of the Empire."

The flow into Magnus's throat had stopped for a moment. It began again.

"Yes, Magnus, swallow. You will be my slave, my toilet, my woman. I shall pierce your nipples and the head of your shaft and parade you naked through the banquet halls and orgy rooms of the Imperial House. You will kneel beside me in my box at the coliseum, and when my bladder is full you will relieve me with your mouth; and when my shaft is hard you will lie on your back with your legs in the air and beg me to fuck you while my courtiers look on and laugh.

"When you displease me, I shall beat you. When you fawn and beg for mercy, I shall slap you for your insolence. And all Rome shall see. Women will blush to think that they once desired you, and men who once envied you will look upon you with loathing and disgust. Eventually you will come to bore me, and I will allow any man who wishes it, from the lowest beggar to my greatest general, to take you in the mouth and ass, to beat you, piss in you, punish your nipples and shaft; and many men will proudly boast of their triumph over Magnus, who was once so famous and powerful, who is now nothing more than the bruised and battered plaything of the Emperor Marcellus.

"You will be physically altered, against your will. Already there is something soft and womanish about you. That is why I had the hair stripped from your body. Do you know the legend of the Jews, of their hero named Samson? He was a mightier man than you, Magnus, and he was brought low when he was shorn of the hair on his head. There is always a kernel of truth even in the most ludicrous of these Oriental tales; and the Jews were right, to a point—except that it is not the hair on a man's head that you remove to make him docile and weak, but the hair on his body and around his sex.

"Eventually I shall take you much further than that. You are still too muscular and heavy. That will change after I have you gelded. One night, when the world weighs heavy upon me and I desire a special amusement, I shall have the Nubians crucify you and slice off your testicles, and Urius and I shall eat them before your eyes.

"After that we will hardly need to shave you. The hair will grow sparse on your body and face. The powerful muscles of your shoulders and limbs will dwindle and soften. Your great bellowing voice will grow high and lisping. Men will see you and scarcely believe that you were once Magnus the gladiator.

"You will still amuse me, for a time; but finally you will become too pathetic to arouse any man. And that is when you shall die upon my shaft. I shall watch your body writhe and convulse, savor the grip of your throat as you struggle for air and bring me to climax. The last thing you will know of this world will be the hardness of my shaft in your throat, and the look of ecstasy in my eyes. You will look up at me and your eyes will plead for release—and I will give it to you. . . ."

# – Eleven –

"Kill me now!"

Those had been Magnus's words, his plea, when Marcellus had finally finished his profane litany, gently pushing Magnus away from his shaft, rubbing it wet and glistening over the clean-shaven face held tight between his thighs—then shoving him to the floor with sudden violence and erupting into a convulsion of laughter.

Marcellus's words had been the words of a man loosened by wine and drunk with the power of his own erection, lulled by the intoxication of sex into weaving a web of obscene fantasy and unspeakable desires. Even Magnus had been seduced by the horrific visions of his own destruction, painted before his eyes by the senator's smooth monotone, a compelling voice that spoke so calmly not of what might be, but of what had to be, of the inevitable triumph of Marcellus and the ultimate debasement of his slave. The heat and fullness of Marcellus's sex in his mouth pacified Magnus, the surge of the man's urine was strangely narcotic, and Magnus felt himself consumed by a power and a vision that could not be contested.

It was the laughter that unnerved him, that drew him back to the moment. His mouth emptied, Magnus was suddenly without the comforting focus of the senator's great shaft filling him and pulsing warmly against his lips. In a confused instant, what had been a fantasy woven of darkest silk was abruptly real again, minted of hard steel and beaten gold.

Marcellus's laughter made his blood run cold. If the strangeness of his captor's voice could be explained by the drunkenness of wine and arousal, his laughter was of a different species of monstrosity altogether; Marcellus was mad. And his madness did not mean that his schemes would not succeed—more than one madman had ruled the

*Slaves of the Empire*
Published by The Haworth Press, Inc., 2006. All rights reserved.
doi:10.1300/5502_11

Empire already. Marcellus was not a man to live on fantasies and dark imaginings; he would see them carried out, to the last detail.

"Kill me now!" Magnus had whispered, holding his eyes shut, seeing the future before him with an almost hallucinatory clarity, all the more terrible because he would know with every passing instant what the final end would be.

Magnus bowed his head in sobbing submission. Marcellus owned him now; not only his body, but the blood that coursed through it and the breath that gave it life. There could be no refusal, no bargaining; Magnus could only beg, and pray that a madman might see his way to mercy. He prostrated himself and begged for death.

But the only answer to his broken pleading was more laughter, as Urius joined with Marcellus. The gladiator's low chuckling exposed Marcellus's madness all the more—it was evil but sane, and alongside Marcellus's strange braying it was like the innocent laughter of a child.

Magnus opened his eyes and looked up. Marcellus loomed over him, leaning forward on his throne, one elbow resting on the arm of his chair, the other resting on his knee, assuming the ancient posture of a king sitting in judgment. His face was wholly visible now in the firelight; and the sight of it hovering above him threw Magnus into deeper confusion and greater panic. There was no madness in Marcellus's eyes, only cold determination; no slackness, no drunkenness in the unyielding set of his jaw, only the hardness of infinite cruelty.

Magnus shut his eyes again. "Kill me now, Marcellus," he whispered. "I beg you."

A long silence followed, broken only by the crackling of flames— then a rush of air as Urius wielded the switch, the crack of blistered flesh and a strangling sob wrenched from Magnus's throat.

"You may beg to be whipped. Beg to be beaten. And soon you will beg to be mounted by me, to feel the sweetness of my shaft inside you. But you may never beg for favors from me, Magnus. . . ."

There was a further shattering inside him, and Magnus saw himself as if in a dream made of crystals within crystals, each shell broken and swept away in succession, believing each time that the final core had been reached, only to feel it crack open to expose another, ever more vulnerable breakage within.

They proceeded to use him. His groveling, once begun, seemed only natural and fitting. Magnus was seduced by his own burning humiliation, by something within himself that he had never exposed to any other man; it was their strange intimacy that overwhelmed him. They violated him, each pushing a finger up alongside the tail in his ass, and he did not resist. They were amused by his groveling, and he performed for them. They punished him when he knelt to worship their cocks, slapped him when he opened his mouth wide to be fed, whipped him when he raised his ass and swung the tail in lewd gyrations, begging in silence to be impaled on the flesh of his tormentors. Their harshness and coldness, their surly amusement and condescension only fueled his frenzy.

At last he was mounted upon the platform where he had first taken Eskrill, bound by his wrists and ankles. His eyes were closed, and beyond the darkness, through a fog of pain, came a word, repeated over and over: "Eat . . . Eat . . . Eat . . ." And with each cooing repetition of the word, a vast thickness, fleshy but unyielding, was being pushed into him, feeding itself through his mouth and into his throat, slickly retreating, then filling him again, a great worm of flesh forcing him to ingurgitate its mass and then vomit it whole, over and over until the repetition became all that existed.

The worm pulled itself free. A hand slapped his face. He opened his eyes, dazed and still hungry.

Before him, Marcellus's sex hovered, glossy with saliva, dripping opal from its tip. Always hard, inexhaustible, impossible to satisfy. Marcellus slapped him with it. Magnus groaned. Urius, somewhere nearby, laughed softly.

"I think it is time," Marcellus said in a low voice.

"Yes." It was Urius. "I want to watch as you take him. To see him buck and strain . . ."

Both stood before him then—Urius in his perfect golden beauty, Marcellus in his dark madness. His masters.

"Do you want me to fuck you, Magnus?" The voice came from a great distance above him, muffled but distinct; and Magnus thought, in a moment of strange clarity, that this was how the first men had heard the voices of gods and known that they were not the masters of the world, but the helpless slaves of greater powers.

"Answer me, Magnus. Do you want it? You'll never again be the man you were, once it's been inside you. I've seen it happen too often before. Boys, eunuchs, soldiers, slaves—they are all the same, once it has mastered them. Beg me to fuck you, Magnus. It won't hurt as badly, if you say the words. . . ."

His head wrenched back, Magnus stared at the glistening shaft, rearing rampant and invincible before his face, wet with saliva dredged from deep in his throat. He opened his mouth to speak, but his throat was bent, so battered and bruised within that he choked on the words.

And the world changed.

It began with soft laughter—Urius and Marcellus softly laughing above him—before their laughter twisted weirdly into wailing gasps, then exploded into roaring screams of pain.

Before him their bodies writhed and stiffened, jerked forward and stiffened again in some horrifying, inexplicable spastic dance. They staggered forward, their cocks brushing his face, their hands grasping wildly at his shoulders. They collapsed upon him, convulsing and spattering him with a warm wetness.

Even as they fell to the floor, Eskrill and Erskin continued to stab them. Each boy held a dagger dark with blood. Blood sprayed upon their hands, faces, and chests. The blades swung up and down, flashing in the firelight where steel showed through the coating of red.

When the two men no longer moved, no longer even writhed each time the blades descended, the boys rose from the floor, breathing heavily, covered with sweat and blood.

For a long time Magnus could not speak. They loosened his bonds and lifted him from the platform, staggering under his weight. They carried him, half-dragging him to a place near the brazier.

Erskin took a cloth and wiped his stinging wounds with cool water. Eskrill held a wineskin to his lips, but the liquid was acrid in his throat. He choked and coughed and closed his eyes. A numbing weakness overcame him, until their hands, shaking him, finally brought him back to consciousness.

"What have you done?" he muttered. Then, fully awake, feeling his skin prickle with dread, he shouted. "What in Hades have you done?"

"You said we would die if we tried to escape," Erskin said. His voice was oddly calm. "But at least we will have tried. What is done is done. And it will not be Marcellus and his friend who put us to death." The boy spoke solemnly, without passion. It was not the voice of a slave or a criminal. So princes spoke, in the face of harsh justice and impending crisis.

Magnus stared at the blood-soaked bodies crumpled on the floor and shook his head. "For this they will kill every slave in the household."

"Then they will kill you as well. Help us, Magnus!"

"You fools. You barbarian fools." Magnus raised his hand in anger. Then he saw the determination in the boys' eyes and the daggers still clutched tightly in their fists. He sat back, trying to think.

A sense of Fate, cold and black, settled upon him. In the space of a few hours, his life had been shattered. Now his life was as good as over, as surely as if Marcellus had already made good his threat to strangle him upon his shaft. They would crucify him, along with the boys. The crowds who had cheered him in the arena would come to pelt his body with dung, and to watch the carrion birds consume his entrails.

"Where were you? How did you come here?" he asked in a dull voice.

"The eunuchs were bathing us. They are dead now," Eskrill said. "At the bottom of the pool."

"You drowned them?" Magnus was shocked, remembering the two young eunuchs, so pliant and harmless. Eskrill and his brother were warriors after all, and barbarians. Marcellus had pushed them too far. Would Magnus have had the courage to do the same?

He shook his head wearily, and looked again at the two corpses. It had happened so suddenly, it still seemed unreal. "Where did you think you could escape to?"

"To the North. To our homeland."

"Impossible," Magnus said bitterly.

Then he thought of his chance meeting with Talloc the previous day, and the blackness lifted from his spirit. The chance was small, infinitely small. Still, as long as there was hope at all, he could do better than wait in the cellar to be discovered and killed.

He rose unsteadily to his feet. The boys looked at him curiously, still not quite trusting him.

"How soon will their bodies be discovered?" he asked. "Tonight?"

Erskin shook his head. "No one interrupts Marcellus when he is at his pleasure. No one will enter this room until they are certain that something has happened. Tomorrow at noon, perhaps. Perhaps even later."

"What is the hour now?"

"Five hours till dawn."

Then we may have just enough time, if we take the fastest horses in the stable. If Talloc will take us. If we are not recognized on the way. It will help that I'm clean-shaven. . . . Find some way to remove the bracelets from our throats and wrists, but save them; we will need the gold. Go into the house and find whatever valuables you can. Small things that we can carry—rings and such. And cloaks and tunics, the kind of clothing travelers wear. And food—I've never been so hungry. I'll go with you, to help you bring the eunuch's bodies here, where they won't be found."

"Where are we going?"

"To your homeland, boys."

"And you will help us? You're going there too?"

"There is nowhere in the Empire I can go. For the rest of my life, I will be an exile."

"Our father is a great man. He will reward you, Magnus—"

"Enough of that. Up the stairs!"

"But where—"

"I have a friend, a shipowner who sails from Ostia at dawn, for the East, Byzantium. From there, we might be able to travel North and cross Sarmatia, into the Northern forests. If we are not recognized. If we reach his ship in time. If he will help us. If one of his sailors does not betray us for a bounty. There will be doubt and danger in every moment."

Suddenly Magnus was struck by dread, and he froze. Then he saw the boys' faces. They were frightened, too, and looking to him for courage.

He took Erskin's face in his hands and kissed him. The boy squeezed him tightly.

Magnus broke away and turned to Eskrill. He touched the boy's face and ran his fingers over the welt that stretched from his temple to his chin.

Magnus' throat tightened. He had to take a deep breath before he could speak. "Go on," he whispered hoarsely.

The boys bounded up the steep stairway, taking two steps at a time. Magnus began to follow, then paused. He turned and looked for a long time at the two bodies that lay unmoving beside the fire; then he turned back and ascended the stair.

# ABOUT THE AUTHOR

**Aaron Travis**'s first erotic story appeared in 1979 in *Drummer* magazine. Over the next fifteen years he wrote dozens of short stories, the serialized novel *Slaves of the Empire,* and hundreds of book and video reviews for magazines including *Mach, First Hand, Manscape, Hombres, Advocate Men, Mandate, Blueboy, Studflix,* and *Stroke.* His stories have also been translated into Dutch, German, and Japanese. In 2003, his story "The Hit" was voted their all-time favorite by readers of Susie Bright's Best American Erotica anthology series.

## Order a copy of this book with this form or online at:
### http://www.haworthpress.com/store/product.asp?sku=5502

# SLAVES OF THE EMPIRE

_____in softbound at $12.95 (ISBN-13: 978-1-56023-558-3; ISBN-10: 1-56023-558-6)

*109 pages*

Or order online and use special offer code HEC25 in the shopping cart.

COST OF BOOKS_____

POSTAGE & HANDLING_____
*(US: $4.00 for first book & $1.50*
*for each additional book)*
*(Outside US: $5.00 for first book*
*& $2.00 for each additional book)*

SUBTOTAL_____

IN CANADA: ADD 7% GST_____

STATE TAX_____
*(NJ, NY, OH, MN, CA, IL, IN, PA, & SD*
*residents, add appropriate local sales tax)*

**FINAL TOTAL**_____
*(If paying in Canadian funds,*
*convert using the current*
*exchange rate, UNESCO*
*coupons welcome)*

☐ **BILL ME LATER:** (Bill-me option is good on US/Canada/Mexico orders only; not good to jobbers, wholesalers, or subscription agencies.)

☐ Check here if billing address is different from shipping address and attach purchase order and billing address information.

Signature_____

☐ **PAYMENT ENCLOSED: $**_____

☐ **PLEASE CHARGE TO MY CREDIT CARD.**

☐ Visa ☐ MasterCard ☐ AmEx ☐ Discover
☐ Diner's Club ☐ Eurocard ☐ JCB

Account #_____

Exp. Date_____

Signature_____

Prices in US dollars and subject to change without notice.

NAME_____

INSTITUTION_____

ADDRESS_____

CITY_____

STATE/ZIP_____

COUNTRY_____ COUNTY (NY residents only)_____·_____

TEL_____ FAX_____

E-MAIL_____

May we use your e-mail address for confirmations and other types of information? ☐ Yes ☐ No
We appreciate receiving your e-mail address and fax number. Haworth would like to e-mail or fax special discount offers to you, as a preferred customer. **We will never share, rent, or exchange your e-mail address or fax number.** We regard such actions as an invasion of your privacy.

*Order From Your Local Bookstore or Directly From*
### The Haworth Press, Inc.
10 Alice Street, Binghamton, New York 13904-1580 • USA
TELEPHONE: 1-800-HAWORTH (1-800-429-6784) / Outside US/Canada: (607) 722-5857
FAX: 1-800-895-0582 / Outside US/Canada: (607) 771-0012
E-mail to: orders@haworthpress.com

**For orders outside US and Canada,** you may wish to order through your local
sales representative, distributor, or bookseller.
For information, see http://haworthpress.com/distributors

*(Discounts are available for individual orders in US and Canada only, not booksellers/distributors.)*
PLEASE PHOTOCOPY THIS FORM FOR YOUR PERSONAL USE.
http://www.HaworthPress.com                                                    BOF06